TIED TO YOU

A Wild Side Novel

RILEY HART

Cover Design by X-Potion Designs
Cover Photo by John Karrer
Edited by Prema Editing. Proofread by Nathan at Indigo Marketing and Judy's Proofreading.
Artwork by Sarah Jo Chreene

Dedication

To Devon.
Thank you for dealing with all my craziness
and for being my friend.

PROLOGUE

MILES SORENSON LAY in a bed that wasn't his own. A soft, steady snore came from the man beside him, his arm thrown over his face, his spent cock flaccid in a nest of dark pubic hair. Hair that Miles had felt scratch his face as he'd taken Quinn's dick deep into his mouth—the scent of sex, musk, and man as he'd blown him.

He should get out of this bed right now. It was late Sunday afternoon, and Miles didn't make a habit of hanging around after he fucked someone. He sure as shit didn't make a habit of spending a whole weekend with someone the way he'd done with Quinn the past couple days.

Still, he didn't get up, instead trying to figure out why, other than the fact that Quinn was sexy and a good fuck, he still lay in this bed after meeting up with him late Friday night.

He'd separated from his friends at the corner outside of Wild Side, the bar they met up at every Friday night. But instead of going home, like he usually did, he'd made his way to another bar, where he'd seen a man sitting at a table by himself.

They'd made eye contact, and the second they did, Miles saw the interest in the other man's face. He'd walked right

1

over, sat down with him, and now he was in Quinn's bed two days later, listening to Quinn sleep the most soundly Miles had seen him sleep.

Quinn rolled over and slung his arm over Miles's torso. He only knew the man's first name, the same way Quinn only knew he was Miles. They hadn't bothered with surnames. What was the point? Neither of them planned to see each other past this weekend.

They'd both needed to fuck, done that, and there wasn't much more to the story. Only, they hadn't just fucked, had they? They'd talked too. Not about important shit, but they talked more than Miles spoke to most people other than his best friends, Chance, Oliver, and Matt.

"You're thinking hard," Quinn mumbled into Miles's side. Maybe he wasn't sleeping so soundly after all.

"How do you know that? You met me two days ago, and you can read my moods now?" He spoke with a smile, but it was a serious question. Maybe they'd fucked and talked for two days straight, but they didn't really *know* each other.

"I feel it in your muscles. Your body's tight, and your breathing changes. I pay attention to these things." Quinn sat up, his elbow on the bed, looking down at Miles. He had these soft, compassionate, brown eyes. It was one of the first things Miles had noticed about him when they met in the bar—his kind eyes. Such a fucking cliché—meeting a man at a bar and banging his brains out all weekend.

"Yeah? And I'm pretty sure that's the first time you slept for more than half an hour at a time. I pay attention to shit, too. Wanna talk about that?" Miles cocked a brow at Quinn and saw him frown.

"No, no I don't."

"Didn't think so. Don't call me on my shit, and I won't call you on yours."

"Yes, sir. Jesus, you're a bossy bastard. That is so fucking hot. I sort of want to go ass up for you again."

Miles chuckled. He and Quinn had fit together that way. They both enjoyed the same kind of sex—a little rougher, some spanking, Miles giving and Quinn taking.

The thought made Miles want to play with Quinn's hungry little hole again too. He was something else, that was for sure. But instead of taking Quinn up on his offer he said, "I should go."

"*Finally*," Quinn replied and then winked at him. "I never thought I'd get you out of here. You didn't fall in love with me, did you?"

Miles chuckled. "Fuck no. You didn't fall in love with *me*, did *you*?" he teased back. Something about Quinn brought out a playfulness in him, and there wasn't much that made Miles feel that way.

"No, baby. There's plenty of dick in West Hollywood."

"Yeah, but I know how to lay the good pipe," Miles replied, almost feeling like he was stalling, which was ridiculous. He had no reason to want to hang around.

"You're a fucking machine. I've never had it so good. Although, my head still stings from how hard you pulled my hair." Quinn rubbed a hand over Miles's chest, his white skin a contrast to Miles's darker tone.

"You liked it," Miles countered. He sure as shit had liked it.

"Did I say I didn't?" Quinn replied.

Instead of keeping their teasing going, Miles again said, "I should go."

Quinn nodded and sat up straighter. Miles made his way to the edge of the bed, sitting there with his back to Quinn. His bones felt like they weighed a million pounds. Like he couldn't hold himself up, but then he realized he was being incredibly dramatic for no fucking reason and pushed his ass out of bed and got dressed. There was a rustling sound behind him, and he knew Quinn was doing the same thing.

Five minutes later, they stood at the front door of Quinn's apartment.

"I know the two days weren't really in the plan, but it worked out okay," Quinn told him. He looked tired, like he needed some more sleep.

Miles glanced around the apartment. There were computers and video game shit on an L-shaped desk in the corner. Dishes sat on the kitchen counter. They'd taken breaks between fucking to eat, but that was about all they'd done—fucked, rested, eaten, showered, then repeated the process again and again. Quinn's ass had to be killing him, but they'd opted for blowjobs too. He didn't know how either of them had managed to get it up as many times as they had.

"Yeah, it did work out okay," Miles finally answered him. "Thanks for a good time."

111111

"Thank you for the same thing," Quinn replied. Miles leaned forward and took his mouth one more time—their tongues tangled before Miles took control. When he'd had his taste, he pulled back, winked at Quinn and then walked away.

That had been just the distraction he'd needed.

CHAPTER ONE

MILES COULD FEEL Quinn's eyes on him from the bar. He tried to ignore him while listening to Matt, Oliver, and Chance joke and tease each other. They'd finally dropped the conversation about Miles's sex life, which they'd been annoyingly focused on when they discovered Quinn staring at him. What they didn't realize was that Miles had met him before. He'd had him before—more than once. Matt, though…he kept glancing Quinn's way, then back at Miles again. He had a feeling Matt could tell Miles knew him, even though he'd blown off the question when Matt asked it.

And realistically, he couldn't say he *knew* Quinn. They'd met, then spent a weekend fucking and talking about random shit before parting ways. It had been months since he'd seen the other man. He also didn't know why he didn't want his friends to know he'd slept with Quinn. It wasn't as though he was ashamed of hooking up. It wasn't as if they didn't know he did it. Maybe it was the fact that he and Quinn had been together more than once…that Miles had spent a weekend fucking his brains out. A weekend his friends had no knowledge of.

Jesus, their group was close. Maybe they shared a little too much…but if it weren't for them, Miles wouldn't share anything with anyone.

"You okay, baby?" Chance asked from beside him.

Miles nodded and looked at him. "Yes. Why wouldn't I be okay?"

"Because Oliver said your name three times and you stared into space like you were dead inside?" he asked. Their friends laughed, and Miles rolled his eyes. Fucking Chance.

"Sorry. Spacing out. And I *am* dead inside, remember? Big, bad, mean Miles." His friends always gave him shit because Miles believed in brutal honesty. He ran off logic, where Oliver ran off his heart, Chance his dick—and maybe his love of life—and Matt, well, Matt ran off music and Oliver.

Miles would always be the one who told it as it was and maybe came off as a bit of a dickhead sometimes.

Oh well. There was no changing him now, and he was fine with that.

"So what did you want?" Miles asked, giving Oliver his attention. He'd been friends with Ollie and Chance all his life. They were the only people he let himself depend on, which likely made him even more of an asshole. Matt came along not long after they hit double digits in age. Oliver had been in love with Matt since then and the two of them just recently committed to each other.

Miles hadn't liked it at first. He'd been sure Matt would hurt Ollie, but now? Well, Matt won his cold, little heart over. Congrat-u-fucking-lations.

"I don't remember," Oliver answered his question.

"See? I just knew it wasn't anything important." Miles winked at them before taking the last swallow of his whiskey. He'd always been a whiskey kind of man.

"Everything I have to say is important," Oliver teased.

"Then don't forget what it is," Miles tossed back at him.

Not too far from their table, one of the Wild Side dancers shook his ass from his perch on one of the raised squares throughout the bar. Each one had a different man on it. Chance danced here on Saturday and Sunday nights, but unless he picked up an extra Friday, it was one night he always had off.

The dancer winked at him. They came to Wild Side often enough that Miles knew his name was Julio.

"Ooh, looks like J has his eyes on you," Chance said. "Christ, why the fuck is everyone hot for you tonight?"

"Because they all want my big cock." Miles grinned, but all Chance's words did was remind him that Quinn was here, sitting at the bar, watching him. "You know what they say…"

"Yes. Once you go black, you never go back. You've re-minded us of that ever since you went all *masc top* at seventeen." Chance eyed him like he dared Miles to argue with him, and Miles would.

"I resent that. I might be primarily a top, but I don't play that *masc* shit. I just happen to like giving the D and know I have a big one."

The men at the table erupted in a combination of laughter or giving Miles shit. He tossed a glance over his shoulder, saw that Quinn had his back to him and was talking to another man who sat beside him.

Huh.

The guy reached over and touched Quinn's shoulder and laughed. It was obvious he was interested, the way he angled his body toward Quinn's. Not that Miles could blame him. He truly was sexy as hell—tall, though shorter than Miles, with dark brown hair that was longer on the top and cut close to his head on the sides. It was styled, so it stuck up, messily but if it were wet, it would hang over his forehead.

He had smooth, clear skin, dimples when he smiled and had these thick fucking lips that Miles had thoroughly enjoyed seeing wrapped around his cock.

He turned back toward his friends and signaled the waitress over for another drink, wishing he didn't wonder if Quinn was still having trouble sleeping, or why he did. It had been pretty obvious the weekend Miles stayed with him that it was some kind of issue for him. They'd had that in common...not that Miles didn't sleep well—but he thought that sometimes, they both just needed someone to take the loneliness away. Although Quinn would admit it out loud when Miles wouldn't.

He had also had no doubt Quinn must have a good reason, and that was another thing Miles didn't have.

QUINN LAUGHED AT the joke from his new friend, who sat beside him. Billy, he thought the other man said his name was.

They'd started up a conversation when Dare, the bar owner, had stopped by to see how they were doing. Quinn had never been here before, but the guy seemed incredibly passionate about his bar and had somehow known it was Quinn's first time at Wild Side.

Billy had cut in then and joked about how not a damn thing went down in Wild Side that Dare didn't know about, even someone visiting for the first time, and from there, Dare had gone back to work, while Billy and Quinn chatted.

It had been a little while now, and even though he appreciated Billy's conversation, he was ready to get out of here. He liked to have a good time, always had, but he wasn't typically the guy who went out to a club or bar to find said good time.

Today, his apartment had felt too empty. Too quiet. Quinn didn't always love the quiet, and though he had a lot of friends he could go out with, he typically didn't. It had always been his best friend, Christian, who was now back and forth between California and Virginia with his guy.

But Quinn had always been…particular on whom he got close to, and though Billy seemed like a nice enough guy, Quinn wasn't sure he'd do it for him tonight.

He let his eyes make their way back toward Miles. There were three other men with him at the table. Quinn assumed two of them were his best friends who Miles had told him about. He hadn't said much about them—just that he had two men he'd been friends with his whole life, and they met up with each other every Friday night, but he hadn't said where.

Quinn guessed the third man was the boyfriend of one of them. Either that or they were a really handsy group of friends.

"Is that an ex or something?" Billy asked, pulling Quinn out of his thoughts.

"Who?" he questioned even though he knew damn well who Billy was talking about.

"The black guy at the table. You keep looking his way, and he keeps staring at you too."

He fucking knew it. Miles gave him a look that said he somehow thought Quinn was spying on him but the motherfucker couldn't keep his eyes off Quinn either.

Not that he could blame him. Quinn knew he was a good piece of ass, and they'd had a whole lot of fun the weekend they shared together.

"Or something," Quinn answered Billy's question. "Sorry."

"Don't be. I was just being friendly. I wasn't looking to fuck you. You're nice to look at, but I have someone."

Oh…well, now he felt like an asshole. "I apologize again. I obviously just assume everyone wants to fuck me," he teased, hoping not to make himself look like such a jerk. "I usually carry a stick. It comes in handy, fighting off all the men who want me."

Billy laughed, and then Quinn felt the hairs on the back of his neck rise. He was aware that was the most ridiculous thing in the world to think, but he knew when he looked up, Miles's eyes would be on him.

He'd be lying if he didn't admit he wanted his on Miles as well—so Quinn found him, saw him make his way through a crowd of bodies and toward the bathroom.

Miles's whiskey-colored stare met him for one hot, explosive second before he turned and kept moving. There wasn't a chance Quinn could sit this one out, so he said his goodbyes to Billy, pushed to his feet, and made his way toward Miles.

There was a dull tingle at the base of his spine as he moved through the bodies. Something about Miles felt forbidden, though he couldn't put his finger on what it was. Maybe it was because Miles was so outspoken about certain things but mostly kept himself locked tight. Or maybe it was because Quinn somehow felt like he saw a piece of himself in Miles, even though neither of them had shared anything deep enough for them to know if that was true or not.

Or maybe it was just because he was a hell of a fuck and he'd slipped away from his friends for some reason, and Quinn didn't know what it was.

He made it almost all the way to the end of the hallway where the restrooms were when a hand wrapped around his bicep.

There was a little indention in the wall, a small space that Miles had ducked into and now was pulling Quinn there with him.

"Did I tell you I meet my friends here every Friday night?" he asked.

Quinn chuckled. Jesus, Miles was a cocky bastard. Like Quinn had nothing better to do with his time than to go to a bar just to see Miles? "Do you think I'm stalking you? I mean, there was that one time I sat outside your bedroom window, but…"

He saw a small smile tease Miles's lips. His skin was a rich brown, his eyes a shade or two lighter. He had a square jaw and buzzed black hair, and a thick, muscular body that Quinn had quite enjoyed. If he was honest, he wouldn't mind enjoying it again.

"You would have to know where I live for that," Miles replied.

"But I'm a stalker remember? Hell, maybe I knew everything about you before you even walked into the bar that first night…or maybe it was a coincidence as is tonight. There are only so many gay bars, even in West Hollywood, and even if I knew you came here, doesn't mean I couldn't come without it being for you."

"You came a lot for me that weekend." His voice was deep and smooth as honey.

"Check you out, trying to distract me from the fact that you came down this hallway hoping I'd follow. Why don't we cut to the chase and you tell me where to meet you tonight?" He'd learned during the one weekend they spent together that Miles always cut to the chase, and Quinn had no problem doing that as well.

He could have sworn he saw a bloom of desire burst in Miles's eyes, and damned if his dick didn't like that. He'd always had a weakness for pretty, distant boys.

"You think so, huh?" Miles asked.

"Are you really going to pretend otherwise? I didn't figure you the type."

"What type is that?" Miles questioned.

"Coward," he replied, hoping to get what he wanted. He

wasn't sure what it was about Miles that intrigued him so much—or maybe it wasn't intrigue and just horniness. Or a combination of the two.

Miles's lips stretched into a thick grin. "Remember, *I* really do know where *you* live. Be there in an hour." And then he pushed his way around Quinn and disappeared into the crowd again.

CHAPTER TWO

The Weekend

"*T*HIS IS FUCKING *stupid.*" *Miles pushed out of bed, Quinn's beige, patterned blanket getting tangled around his feet. Roughly he kicked out of it, went to the en suite attached to Quinn's room, took a quick piss, and washed his hands. He took longer than need be, stalling, of course, but seriously, what the fuck was this? Why was Quinn asking him shit like this? He turned the faucet off before turning around to see a naked Quinn leaning against the headboard. They'd spent most of the weekend naked like that. It's what their time together was about, after all.*

Quinn's dick wasn't hard. It lay soft, against his thigh. The man had a sexy fucking body, long, lean with defined muscles. His small, dark brown nipples were hard, his skin pale, chest and face both smooth. Those fucking lips, though. Jesus, Miles had never seen anything like it. He wanted them wrapped around the root of his cock.

"You're weird," he finally said, fully aware that he probably could have come up with a better reply than that. Damn it. He hated feeling off his game.

"No, I'm drunk. You're the one who had me pull out that bottle of Patrón. Alcohol makes me a talky fucker."

Quinn seemed to always be a talky fucker. The alcohol was a shitty excuse.

"And maybe it is stupid, but you're going to humor me because you'll likely want to fuck me again."

Well...he had Miles there... "Oh I am, am I?"

"Yes, you are."

"Can we not pretend you don't want it just as much as I do? I can have you begging for it in no time flat." He wasn't exaggerating either. They both liked it when Quinn begged.

"Yeah, I love your cock, but I'm also a stubborn motherfucker. You give me what I want; then we'll both get what we want." Quinn crooked his finger at Miles, calling him over like they were in a cheesy movie or something. He couldn't help but smile.

Miles had no idea how they'd gone from just fucking to Quinn attempting to really talk to him, but they seemed to be there. This sure as hell wasn't typically how his hookups went.

None of those other nights turned conversations beyond "top or bottom? I only fuck with a Jimmy, and poppers don't fly with me."

But then Quinn gave him a drunk, dopey smile and he found himself asking, "What was the question again?" even though he knew it. He leaned against the dresser, with his arms crossed, and waited. He wasn't supposed to be the one doing what Quinn said. It was supposed to be the other way around.

"Tell me something you wish you had the balls to do, but don't."

Miles rolled his eyes. "Nothing. If I want to do something, I do it." He just wasn't a guy who wanted much. Anything he could desire, he had. Well, that wasn't true, was it? There was one thing he sometimes wished he could do but he never would. It was a foolish dream, anyway.

"You're thinking. I can see the wheels turning... Do I want to tell Quinn this or not? Will I still be the gorgeous as fuck, brooding dude who oozes sex, if I say something that really matters? The answer is yes, by the way."

Goddamn Quinn. Miles began to crack a smile. He shook his head, sighed and said, "I'm serious. If I want something, I do it. Why deny myself?"

Quinn frowned, then rolled his eyes. "Fine. I'll come up with a different question. Hmmm." He tapped his forehead and Miles found himself smiling again. Quinn was so fucking ridiculous. He never saw himself enjoying it but then, it was for one weekend so why not?

"I got it. This is a good one. You're going to hate me for it."

"And that's good?" Miles asked.

"It's fun."

"You're crazy."

"You're trying to distract me, and I won't fall for it. Tell me something about yourself that no one else knows."

Miles shook his head. "Getting a little deep, aren't we? Plus, I would have nothing to tell you, even if I wanted to. My friends know everything there is to know about me. If they didn't, why would I tell you? Someone I don't really know."

Quinn cocked a brow at him. "For the very reason you just said, sexy. Because you don't know me. You'll never see me again. There's a safeness in that. You can say something without having to worry about what the other person thinks because to you, I'm nothing but some guy you spent a weekend fucking."

Those words rubbed at Miles's skin in a strange way. They shouldn't. That's exactly who Quinn was to him. Now he was the one being ridiculous.

But then…there was a part of what Quinn said that made sense. He wouldn't have to look Quinn in the eyes again. He wouldn't have to wonder what he thought of him. And even in the short amount of time that Miles had known Quinn, it was obvious he didn't give up easily. He would pester Miles until Miles told him what he wanted to know. Either that or their weekend would be over.

Miles's dick wasn't ready for the weekend to be over. Maybe there was another small part of him that wasn't ready either.

"I can't think of anything," he finally answered.

"Think harder."

"Aren't I supposed to be the bossy one here?" He was pretty sure they both liked it that way.

"Again, then tell me what I want to know and then make me be your good boy."

Desire pricked along Miles's skin. He wanted that. He really fucking wanted it.

Miles thought for a moment, even though he really didn't need to. He knew exactly what he would say…and it might feel good too. Feel good to tell someone who didn't know his past or understand the why of it.

"When I was younger, I used to sneak out of my house and take a bus downtown, skid row, places like that. When I turned sixteen and didn't have to sneak out, I would take my car, but I

never told anyone where I was going."

His words sounded hollow like they echoed somehow. He couldn't believe they were coming out of his mouth at all.

Quinn's brows pulled together. He was obviously trying to figure Miles out—the same way Miles was trying to figure out why he was really telling Quinn this.

"What would you do there?"

Miles took a deep breath and looked toward the floor. "Walk. I would walk up and down areas the homeless frequented. I would look at all the people. Look at their faces. Their eyes. Sometimes I would bring them food. Other times I would just walk...watch." Search.

"That doesn't sound very safe."

Was it Miles or was there a scratchiness to Quinn's voice that hadn't been there before?

"They're just people, and I'm obviously fine."

"I know they're just people. I'm the last person you have to remind of that."

There was a story there, in Quinn's voice and what he said, the same way there was a story behind what Miles was saying. They wouldn't share them, though. Miles knew he wouldn't and didn't believe Quinn would either.

Quinn's hand moved to his crotch, then. It wasn't meant to be sexual, his finger so fucking close to his dick, but it was sexual as hell for Miles. His prick started to get hard.

Quinn's eyes caught his. His brows rose, as if in question, likely seeing the desire in Miles's stare. He was done talking. He hadn't come here to talk.

"Enough talking." Miles walked over to the bed, stood beside Quinn. *"You sore?"* he asked.

"Little bit."

He'd already taken Quinn twice today.

"Then I guess I get your dick in my mouth."

"What if I want yours in mine?" Quinn asked.

"Maybe I'll let you later. Right now, I get what I want."

Quinn's cock filled with blood and a smile grew on those sexy fucking lips of his.

Miles kneeled on the bed and got to work, trying to forget what he'd just told Quinn and how it almost made him feel connected to him.

CHAPTER THREE

M ILES SAT IN his car in front of Quinn's apartment and reconsidered going in. He didn't like how Quinn had assumed he wanted to hook up with him again and now here he was, sitting outside of Quinn's place proving him right.

Then he remembered he'd get an orgasm out of the deal, and hell, who didn't want an orgasm? Of course, he wanted to hook up with Quinn again, so Miles stepped out of his black Lexus, hit the lock on his key fob, and made his way toward the building.

He'd been the first one to bow out of Wild Side tonight, which was unusual. He had no doubt his friends knew he was leaving to meet up with someone. They probably even assumed it was Quinn by the way they'd looked at each other all night, but it was only Matt who he still thought might know that Miles had met him before. Even if he hadn't asked, the way he'd looked at Miles curiously told him that.

It shouldn't matter if he was heading over to fuck someone he already had before. He didn't know why it did, and maybe in some ways, it didn't. He was making a big deal out of things he shouldn't worry about which wasn't usually the way Miles worked. Fucking Quinn.

So he forced those thoughts aside, concentrated on his dick, lifted his arm and knocked on the door. He hardly pulled his hand away before it pulled open.

"I didn't think you'd show," Quinn said.

Yeah, he hadn't been sure either, but he didn't like that Quinn thought the same thing. It felt too close. Or fuck, like he was predictable. "Why would I skip out on sex?"

It was a good question. One he'd asked himself when he considered not coming.

Quinn stepped aside, and Miles entered the apartment. "I highly doubt I'm the only man you could have gotten sex from tonight," Quinn answered and damn it, Miles didn't like the reply.

There was the truth at why this bothered him. Quinn *wasn't* the only person he could fuck. He could have picked up someone else at Wild Side. He could have gone home with Julio or hit up Grindr or Scruff. He didn't have to leave and meet up with the guy he'd spent a weekend with months before. He didn't have to go down a hallway, knowing Quinn would follow and that they'd possibly end up right where they were.

"Eh," Miles shrugged as he heard the door close behind him. "You're easy, and I know you're good." That's what he was going with.

Quinn chuckled. "Well, that's true. My ass is a thing of miracles, and my mouth is fucking incredible too. I'm just as good with my dick, but you know from experience, I'd rather bottom."

Miles cocked a brow at him. "And you know from experience, I'd rather top."

"You want a drink?" Quinn asked.

"I want your ass," Miles replied.

"You'll get it."

Miles watched as Quinn walked into his kitchen. He grabbed a bottle of scotch off the counter. As he poured two glasses, Miles looked around the apartment. It looked exactly how it did the last time he was here—the L-shaped desk, multiple computers and equipment, and Miles knew he had another desk with even more in his bedroom.

There was a T-shirt on the back of his dark blue couch. Multiple video game systems were hooked up to the TV mounted to his wall. He had framed images of video games he'd created on his walls. Two glasses and a plate rested by his computer.

"Do you work from home?" Miles found himself asking as Quinn handed him a drink. He swished the liquid around in the glass as he waited for Quinn to reply.

"Yes and no. I have an office downtown, but I spend a lot of time working, so I do a lot from here, as well." Quinn carried his glass and the bottle with him as he walked over to the couch. He set both down on the coffee table, then lowered down to the couch.

Miles sighed, almost asked why they were sitting instead of screwing, but instead found himself following and taking a seat beside him. Something felt a little off with Quinn tonight, and he didn't know what it was. The strange part was, he didn't only get the feeling from Quinn, he felt it himself as well. This felt…comfortable. Familiar. "Your apartment looks like it's lived in by a fourteen-year-old kid." Miles took a long swallow of the scotch. It tasted good—a sweet burn to it, so he took another drink. Quinn did the same.

"I can only guess what your place looks like… Hmmm." He poured more of the dark brown liquid into his glass and then sat back against the couch. "I'm going to go with dark…not *vampire dark* but brooding, I-have-no-heart dim."

Miles chuckled. Damn it. He was pretty close. "Go on."

Before he spoke again, he drank more of his scotch. Miles watched his throat move as he swallowed, and damn, it made him even more eager to have his dick in Quinn's mouth. He'd let Quinn play a little before he ravaged him.

"I bet you don't have a lot of personal items on display— no pictures of friends or family, nothing that shows what you're passionate about. What are you passionate about, by the way?"

"I'm a lawyer," he admitted. He couldn't remember if he'd shared that with Quinn before. "I like things in order. I'm passionate about control and sex. Are we on a dating site, here? This would be where I'd mention long walks on the beach and shit like that?" If those things appealed to Miles, that was.

"You probably hate the beach." There was a glint in Quinn's eyes that said he was teasing.

"I do not hate the beach. I look good in a Speedo." But he did kind of hate the beach. He just didn't want Quinn to know that.

Quinn's eyes darted down at Miles's dick. "I have no doubt you do."

Quinn emptied his glass. Miles put his to his lips and did the same. The energy in the room changed. It snapped with electricity as he saw Quinn's kind eyes haze over with lust. This was it. This was what he came here for.

"You want it, don't you?" Miles asked and then cupped his bulge. Damn if Miles didn't want it too. His cock hardened, already aching with the need to squeeze inside Quinn's tight ass. "Tell me you want it, Quinn."

"You know I do, you cocky son of a bitch. You know how to lay the good pipe, remember?"

Miles lost count of how many times he'd chuckled since he'd come here. He plucked the glass from Quinn's hand and then set them both on the coffee table. The second he did, their mouths clashed together like two magnets, their opposite poles too close to deny the connection.

Their teeth clanked together. Quinn wrapped his arms around Miles, and Miles threaded his fingers through Quinn's hair, tugging on it the way he remembered Quinn liking.

They were fast and furious. All hunger and need as Miles's tongue pushed into Quinn's mouth and Quinn moaned into Miles's, and goddamn it, he wanted nothing more than to sink his dick deep into Quinn's ass.

He pushed to his feet, his cock so damn hard it hurt. Miles pulled Quinn with him, and their lips attacked one another's again as they made out, stumbling toward the hallway.

Quinn grunted when Miles backed him into the wall. He

laughed against Miles's mouth, and a smile tugged at his own lips. He kissed Quinn deeper, fumbled with the button and zipper on Quinn's pants.

He shoved Quinn's pants down, and Quinn kicked out of them. Miles pulled back enough to push his finger into Quinn's mouth. He sucked it with all he had and then let it go, and Miles slipped it between Quinn's ass cheeks. When he rubbed his finger against Quinn's tight hole, the other man shuddered against him. "Oh yeah. You're starving for my cock, aren't you?" He pushed the tip of his finger inside the first ring of muscle and then pulled it out again and rubbed Quinn's pucker.

"Fuck yes... I've always had a weakness for pretty boys with big cocks."

Quinn was a couple of inches shorter than him, thinner. Miles wrapped an arm around him. Pulled him close. Quinn's legs immediately wrapped around Miles's waist as he lifted him. Their mouths went at each other's again—kissing, licking, sucking, biting like they were both wild animals, and were each other's prey.

Miles pushed his finger inside Quinn again, fucked him with it as Quinn grunted and dropped his head back. Miles went at his throat, sucked the meaty spot where his neck met his shoulder and then teased it with his teeth.

Quinn trembled. Miles looked down and saw his thick cock leaking and wished they were in the position where he could swipe at the pre-come with his tongue.

He began to move then, walked toward Quinn's room

before they both lost their nut. He rubbed his finger against Quinn's hole, petting it like Quinn was his good boy and Miles was giving him his reward.

He turned into Quinn's room, and his legs hit Quinn's bed. He leaned over, tried to drop Quinn onto it, but the other man didn't let go. Miles went down on top of him and damn it, why the fuck hadn't he taken the time to remove his pants too?

He made the motion to pull away and take care of business, but Quinn clutched him, dropped his head back and said, "Play with my hole again. Please," he let out breathlessly.

Miles groaned, almost came in his pants. He'd forgotten how much Quinn loved having his ass played with. During the weekend they'd spent together, when Miles didn't have his cock in him, Quinn at least wanted a finger. He liked his ass red and burning after a good spanking, too.

"I forgot how hungry your ass was for it," he said and then sucked on his own finger before pushing it deep in Quinn.

His eyes rolled back in his head, and Miles smiled because, fuck, he loved getting that response out of a lover. Loved knowing he was making someone lose their mind with pleasure.

He pushed his finger in deep, rubbed Quinn's prostate and then devoured his mouth again. Quinn grunted and moaned, grinding his body against Miles's clothed one, and again, he wished like hell he were naked.

He thrust against Quinn, rubbed his jean-covered dick against the other man, and then he felt Quinn's body tense up.

"Oh fuck...*fuck*." Quinn pulled back, bit his lip, and shot his load between their bodies, come sticking to both Quinn's shirt and Miles's.

"Shit...I'm sorry..." Quinn's breathing was choppy as he released his hold on Miles. "I didn't mean to do that. I thought I could hold it off."

Okay, so that hadn't been the way Miles thought it would go down either, but he grinned at the fact that Quinn was so hungry for him. "Jesus, I'm fucking good," he teased.

Quinn's eyes slipped closed before they fluttered open again. "So fucking good. You're like the king of sex. How did I ever get by without you?"

"Fucker." Miles pulled back.

"Don't go anywhere. Come here, and I'll suck you off...or roll me over and have your turn at my ass."

He had no doubt Quinn would go for it, and there was nothing Miles wanted more at this moment than a piece of Quinn's ass. But there was also no way in hell he was fucking Quinn unless he was sure he could get Quinn off again.

"I'll give you a few minutes to recuperate, easy trigger."

"Fuck you. I don't usually do that. It's been a while for me." Quinn's eyes fluttered, but then he opened them again as he moved to lie the correct way in the bed. "Gimme twenty, and I'll be good to go."

Miles stood and rolled his eyes, but there was a smile on his face too. "I'll be back." He still grinned as he walked into Quinn's bathroom and closed the door. He'd be lying if he didn't admit that felt good, getting Quinn off so easily...not quite as good as coming, but he'd do that when he took Quinn's ass.

Miles took a quick piss then pulled his shirt off. There was a wet spot from Quinn's come. He rinsed it in the sink then let it hang on the rack before he washed his hands, opened the door, and… "Motherfucker."

He knew even from the distance that Quinn had passed out, leaving Miles's cock hard and begging for the release he knew Quinn could give him. How the fuck could he have fallen asleep?

"Goddamn it." Miles walked over to the bed and climbed in. "Quinn," he said softly. He really, really wanted to fuck him. "Hey…sleepy head." He rubbed a hand down Quinn's ass, squeezed the tight globe.

Quinn groaned. His lids twitched and…he looked peaceful. It was strange because Quinn was so light, silly, not at all serious the way Miles was, but looking at him now, at the softness to his face and the way his lips were relaxed, and he knew Quinn was getting something he needed. Something he needed more than Miles needed to come.

"You owe me," he said softly, then found himself touching a strand of Quinn's hair, before he moved to stand up.

"No…" whispered past Quinn's lips, so damn soft, he wasn't sure he heard it. When he added an even quieter, "Don't go…" before his arm wrapped around Miles's waist and he pulled himself closer, Miles realized he'd actually spoken. And that he was still asleep.

He remembered the weekend they spent together. Remembered how Quinn didn't sleep much. How they would fall asleep at the same time, in random hours of the day or night, but Quinn would always wake up before him. When Miles didn't sleep himself, Quinn never slept over half an hour or so at a time.

Yet, that whole weekend, Quinn hadn't asked him to stay or held him like this.

There was a part of him that wanted to go, that itched to get the hell out of his bed, but he didn't. He turned to reach for the lamp, killing the lights, and Quinn's grip on him tightened. He mumbled, groaned, and Miles said, "Shh. I'm not going anywhere. I'm just turning out the light."

Quinn relaxed, but Miles didn't. He lay there in the dark and wondered what in the hell he was doing.

CHAPTER FOUR

The Weekend

*M*ILES SLEPT LIKE *the dead.*

    He lay on his stomach with his left arm over his head, facing Quinn. It wasn't the first time they'd both attempted to pass out from sexual exhaustion. Only Miles really slept, while Quinn typically only closed his eyes and rested.

    He was fairly good at feigning sleep—or not letting himself fully succumb so that he could at least rest his body. When he was in moods like this, lost in his past, it was hard for him to sleep alone.

    The problem was, it was also difficult for him to truly let go with someone he didn't trust enough to allow himself what his body so badly needed.

    Damned if he did and damned if he didn't.

    The hardest part? There was no rhyme or reason to it. There wasn't a pattern or something that triggered him to set him off. It was just the way his body worked.

    Quinn softly brushed his fingers over Miles's shoulders, but the other man didn't move.

    Damn it. He could feel his body succumbing, feel it reaching for what was just out of reach. If Miles could make him come again, maybe it would be enough to push him over that edge.

He was...different. Nothing this weekend had gone the way Quinn thought it would when Miles walked into the bar.

Sexually, he was exactly what Quinn wanted—dominant, bossy top who knew his way around a man's body.

But there were secrets in there, too. Secrets Quinn found himself curious about.

Why did he walk around skid row? Why did he search out the homeless?

And how in the fuck had Quinn gotten Miles to share that with him?

He hadn't expected it. He would have continued fucking Miles even if he hadn't shared something with Quinn because he wanted sex and exhaustion just as badly as Miles did.

But Miles had told him, and now Quinn couldn't stop thinking about it.

Miles groaned, rolled on his side, and pulled Quinn closer.

It wasn't something he would have done if he were awake. It felt...too close, but Quinn let him. He felt Miles's breath on his cheek, and somehow, Miles's rhythmic breathing made his eyes get heavier. Quinn closed them, hoping for what he needed but unsure if he would get it.

It wasn't long before darkness took him deeper and deeper. A voice in his head told him to be cautious because he didn't know Miles very well, but his body just felt too comfortable. He thought about Miles with the homeless again, and that was the last thing he remembered before he lost himself to sleep.

QUINN COULD TELL the sun was out before he opened his eyes. Still, the burn came as a surprise when his lids fluttered open before closing again. Jesus, he drank too much last night. He'd always been a bit of a lightweight. With what he had at Wild Side coupled with what he'd drunk with Miles…

Oh fuck.

There was warm skin against his hand. A body beside him. They'd stumbled into the room planning to fuck…he'd come too early and… "Shit," he groaned before pulling away from Miles.

"You snore," Miles's deep, scratchy voice said beside him.

"Yeah, I do that when I'm drunk. Apparently, I'm an early ejaculator when I'm drinking, too. I hope you don't think it's because you're that skilled at fingering an ass." He wanted to turn away from Miles, but he forced himself to look at him. Had he really blown his load before Miles even got inside of him? Then gone and passed out on the guy?

"Oh, so you want to try and bust my balls, huh?" Miles cocked a dark brow at him, and Quinn thought maybe he didn't want to play this game with Miles.

"If I were the blushing type, my cheeks might be red right now." He tried to play it off as though it didn't really bother him, as though he didn't care that he'd come before Miles could fuck him and then ended the night before making Miles lose his mind too. "I'll make it up to you." Miles had slept in his jeans, which couldn't have been very comfortable. Quinn reached for the button and somehow wasn't surprised when Miles's hand shot out and grabbed his wrist.

What did surprise him was what Miles said next. "You have trouble sleeping alone?"

"Fuck," he groaned. He tried to pull away, but Miles still had a hold of his wrist.

"I was drunk, and I passed out."

"You asked me to stay."

Quinn looked him in the eyes, saw questions in Miles's whiskey-colored irises. Even though Miles kept his emotions on lockdown, Quinn could see the curiosity in him. The way he studied those around him, paid attention to them in ways not many people did. He'd seen it the night they met before they left the bar, seen it in the way Miles looked at him the weekend they spent together, at Wild Side last night, and right now in his bed.

He was an answers guy. He wanted to know things, even if he shouldn't. Even if he didn't share them. Even if he didn't share anything of himself.

But then, he did share a few things of himself, didn't he? He'd told Quinn something no one knew about. He'd told Quinn about walking around areas where homeless frequented. What Quinn didn't know was why.

"I asked you to stay because I was too tired to blow you last night and I figured I could make it up to you today," he said.

Miles paused, stared at him, still gripping his wrist. "Lying doesn't suit you. You're too...light and happy for that."

Quinn chuckled to give himself time before he pulled his hand away. "First, that almost sounded like a compliment. You like me, don't you? And second, who's busting whose balls now?"

Miles didn't reply. Didn't move. His gaze held firmly on Quinn and damned if he didn't find it impossible to look away. Miles was commanding that way. Like he wouldn't take no for an answer even if you found a way to refuse him…because denying him felt impossible too. "I have trouble sleeping alone *sometimes.*"

Most of the time he was fine. It pissed him off when he wasn't.

"And you struggled the weekend we were together?"

"Am I on trial for something? At least pretend you're a cop and arrest me first. We can pretend I resist, and you have to use your weapon on me." He reached out and ran his hand over the bulge in Miles's pants.

Miles let Quinn feel him up but still didn't move. He had his shirt off, all that smooth, brown skin on display, stretched across firm muscles.

His dick was hard, but he just continued to eye Quinn, like he knew it would get to him. There were about two seconds during which Quinn was determined to win, but Miles seemed to have a sort of power over him. "I thought you didn't like to talk?"

"I don't."

"Oh, that's only about yourself. You want all up in everyone else's business, though? You're pretty, but you're not that pretty." He pushed out of bed, lying his ass off. Miles was really that fucking gorgeous.

"Tell me."

And bossy. Damn it. He liked Miles's bossiness. "I had a bad night. I'm sorry you got pulled into it, without at least getting an orgasm out of the deal." He walked into the bathroom and started to take a leak. The bed creaked, and then Miles was there, leaning against the doorframe with his arms crossed.

"Do you mind?" Quinn asked.

"No. That's why I walked over here. You were different last night. I could see it when you were drinking on the couch. You would have struggled if I left, and I didn't because you asked me not to. I'd like to know why."

Because staying when asked wasn't like Miles. Quinn didn't need Miles to say those words for him to know they were true.

Quinn finished pissing and began washing his hands. The weekend they spent together, he'd been the one pushing for more information on Miles, not the other way around, and still, nothing he'd asked was like this. He was asking for real information—the why of something. Quinn didn't ask the why of Miles spending time with the homeless community on the down low. "You really just like to put shit out there, don't you? At least when it comes to someone other than yourself."

"True," Miles answered simply. "It's a wonder anyone can put up with me. Most people don't. I'm brooding, and a little mean, and tell it as it is."

The thing was, Quinn didn't think Miles was mean at all. He thought maybe Miles wished he was or wanted people to believe he was. The why of it, he didn't know.

"Coffee," he replied and shuffled over to his dresser. Quinn pulled out a pair of sweats, slipped them on, and left his room for the kitchen. As he went, he knew Miles didn't follow him right away. Was he giving Quinn a moment? Giving himself one? Likely a little of both.

The thing was, this was new territory for Quinn. He was generally a happy guy. He liked to have fun and enjoy life so telling someone why he sometimes had trouble sleeping wasn't typically something he had to deal with—especially because he didn't struggle with it every day.

The strangest part for him? He was normally extremely picky about the people he let his guard down with enough to sleep beside them. For years when he got into funks like this, he used his best friend Christian. There was no one in the world he trusted more. Chris knew Quinn's past, and he was there for Quinn when he needed him. Christian being in a committed relationship and spending half his time on the other side of the country made things a little harder now. He highly doubted Christian's boyfriend would understand if Quinn flew to Virginia and climbed into bed with them— though it would be fun.

He didn't understand why he felt at ease enough with Miles. It had surprised him during their weekend together and surprised him even more last night. In some ways, he felt like a kindred spirit even though Quinn didn't know much about him.

And he still wasn't sure how much he was willing to tell Miles about himself, either.

CHAPTER FIVE

"HOW DO YOU like your coffee?" Quinn asked him as Miles leaned against the kitchen counter with his arms crossed.

Quinn had his back to Miles. His sweats hung low on his hips, showing the top of his ass crack. He had a gorgeous fucking back. Miles had always had a thing for sexy shoulders and for watching back muscles constrict as someone moved. There was a light dusting of freckles painted across Quinn's, which made them even sexier if you asked Miles. He wanted to taste them, but he kept himself from going over and running his tongue along Quinn's pale skin and instead waited for an answer to a question he wasn't sure why he wanted to know. He damn sure didn't have any right to the information.

"I'll make it." He pushed off the counter and walked across the hardwood floors. "Do you have creamer?"

"Vanilla is in the fridge."

"That works." Miles opened the stainless-steel door and pulled out a container of creamer. He saw the sugar on the counter beside the coffee pot. Once Quinn filled two mugs, they each doctored their own.

Quinn took a sip, his eyes rolled back, and he said, "Good

as an orgasm.”

Miles scoffed at that. “Not an orgasm by me.”

“Oh, look at you, puffing out your chest to show how good you are. I see you, bae.”

Miles frowned. “Bae?”

“Eh. Figured I’d try it out, though I think it’s past its prime. I’m always behind on the cool shit.”

Miles chuckled, then watched as Quinn walked over and sat at the granite table off to the right of his kitchen. “So we’re going to do that, *get to know you* thing, huh? Isn’t that against your rules?” He sat in one of the chairs.

Typically, yes, it was against his rules. Or maybe not rules as much as just not something Miles had ever desired before, but there was a part of him that needed to make sense of this. It was the lawyer in him, needing to know everything. Quinn was such a fun, light, free-spirited man—the complete opposite of Miles, himself—yet he’d needed Miles to stay with him last night. He had a feeling that was the whole reason Quinn had taken Miles home with him that first weekend too. Maybe not to sleep, but so he wouldn’t be alone. To distract him from whatever plagued him.

He could tell Quinn that the last time they were together, he’d shared something with him that no one else knew, but the last thing he wanted was to remind Quinn. It would lead to questions about himself he didn’t want to answer.

When Miles didn’t reply, Quinn asked, “Does that mean you like me? You like me, don’t you? Last time you promised you didn’t fall in love with me.”

Goddamn it. Miles couldn't help the smile that tugged at his lips. Quinn was something else. He enjoyed spending time with him, and that was new for him. He didn't enjoy many people outside of his family, Chance, Ollie, and Matt. "And you're the one who reminded me there's a lot of dick in West Hollywood, yet who did you ask to come home with you again?"

"That wasn't for your dick. It was for your fingering skills, obviously. You were there last night, right?"

Quinn was stalling, but for some reason, Miles let him. "So there's a lot of dick but not fingers?"

"Not as good as yours, baby." Quinn winked at him, and the friendly gesture made Miles's gut flip.

"Why did you want me to stay?"

"Why do you care so much?"

That was a good question, and one Miles planned to dissect at a later date when he was alone. "I'm nosy, now tell me."

"You're cocky and bossy."

"True." Miles knew exactly who he was. He also knew it didn't bother Quinn at all.

Quinn sighed, pushed a hand through his brown hair, making it even more mussed than it had been, before lifting his cup and taking another drink. "You're spoiled and too used to getting your way. I don't know why I feel the need to give it to you. I think you cast some sort of spell on me."

Miles grinned, walked over and cupped Quinn's cheek. His brain told him to keep his distance, but he stood there touching him anyway. "No spell. You just like my cock, and you also enjoy the fact that I'm bossy. You like being told what to do."

Quinn just shrugged. "It can be hot." He sat back, so Miles's hand fell away, groaned and said, "I grew up in foster care. I was kind of a dick back then—angry at the world. Hey, I was like you!" He tried to joke, but Miles didn't respond. He couldn't laugh. His body was too rigid…too tight.

"One home or numerous?"

"More than I can count on both hands," Quinn admitted.

A million questions hammered into Miles's brain—what had happened to Quinn's parents? How old had he been? But he kept his lips tight, refusing to let them open up and try to pluck even more information out of Quinn.

"Some people decided they didn't like me. They waited until I was asleep to show me how much and because of that, sometimes I struggle sleeping alone, but I'm also really fucking picky about who I sleep with. I don't owe you any more than that. Hell, I didn't owe you that much. You should be thankful I like cocky and bossy so much."

He was trying to be funny, but again Miles couldn't laugh. He wasn't sure he could do much of anything right now but concentrate on what Quinn had said to him. A burning sensation started in his stomach and blazed its way up his esophagus. He wished he had his coffee in his hand, so he could take a drink to distract himself and also to kill the taste in his throat.

Quinn was leery who he let his guard down with enough to sleep…yet he'd done it with Miles. Both before and now.

For the first time in his life, he almost wanted to talk, to question. To dig deeper into another person, but there was a stronger part of him that made him take a step back. This made things feel like more than a random fuck, which isn't what either of them needed or wanted.

"I had no right to push you. You didn't owe me anything, and I apologize for forcing the issue. I should go."

Quinn tsked and shook his head. Miles could tell he wouldn't like what was coming next. "Now why doesn't that surprise me?"

What surprised Miles was how he'd had to force himself to speak those words. How he'd had to force himself to say he needed to go. That he felt an unexplainable connection to Quinn from the beginning and those few lines he'd given Miles about his past might explain why. They made Miles feel tangled up, tied to Quinn in a strange way he would likely never admit. He wanted to know more about Quinn, about his story. Wanted to know if there were any similarities to his own.

Miles turned and headed for Quinn's room. Quinn sighed behind him, and Miles knew he had followed.

"It's not a big deal. Don't make it out to be more than it is. It doesn't mean I fell for you and now I'll never be the same without you. Last night was a moment of weakness…and maybe a little post-orgasmic bliss."

Miles pulled his shoes on. "I don't think you fell for me." But things did feel…different. He went into the bathroom, grabbed his shirt, despite the come stain still on it. You could see the spot from Quinn's come and part of the wet area from where Miles had rinsed it.

"So you really did fall for me...wow...I don't know what to say. I appreciate the gesture but—"

Damn it. Miles had to bite back his grin. Why did this man get to him so much? Why were his jokes more endearing than annoying? "I didn't fall for you, and you know it. Stop saying that. I'm leaving because it's time to go."

He pulled his shirt over his head, and Quinn's eyes got big. "Fuck, I really shot."

"That's because no one is as good at pleasuring an ass as I am." And damned if Miles didn't find himself grinning. Fucker. Quinn had him feeling a whiplash of different emotions, and he really didn't understand why.

He groaned because now all he wanted to do was slide those sweats down Quinn's legs and have a go at him again. Instead, he turned and walked through the door.

"Yeah, I remember," Quinn told him. "Then why are you leaving? I owe you an orgasm...or even if you don't want one, I'll be glad to let you give me another."

Miles stopped with his hand on the doorknob, his forehead against the door. "I have to go." Why did he have to leave? And why was it he'd only seen Quinn on two different occasions and both times he had to continually remind himself that he needed to leave?

Without letting himself think about what he was doing, he whipped around, grabbed Quinn's wrist. Pulled him closer, turned them, so Quinn's back was against the door. His mouth went down hard on Quinn's. His tongue pushed past Quinn's lips and tasted coffee and vanilla and fuck, his dick was hard. He gave Quinn a bruising kiss, a possessive kiss because he suddenly felt like he'd lost some of his own control. This was the only way Miles knew how to get it back.

Before he lost his head, pulled Quinn's sweats down, and had him right there by the door, he jerked away. "I have to go." There he was saying that again. Now it was time to follow through.

Quinn stepped aside, and Miles opened the door. He made it partway down the hallway when Quinn called out, "What's your last name?"

Miles stopped...considered not responding...but he did. "Sorenson." Then added, "You?"

"Barker."

It wasn't until Miles heard Quinn's door close that he began walking again. That he let himself admit Quinn intrigued him. That he might like spending time with him. That hearing what Quinn told him, he'd felt like he really had something in common with someone in his personal life, in a way he'd never had with Chase, Matt, or Ollie.

Miles didn't know how to feel about that.

CHAPTER SIX

"YOU LOOK TIRED, Miles. Are you sleeping enough? You're not working yourself to death, are you? Your father does that, though it's not like I have to tell you." His mother stood at the sink, washing vegetables for dinner. She was a beautiful woman. She had platinum blond hair, which was always styled, and crystal blue eyes. Her makeup was always done and her nails always painted. She exercised daily.

She wasn't only beautiful on the outside, but on the inside as well. When Miles was young, she volunteered in his classrooms, and like Chance and Ollie, he always went to the best schools and had the best things. She donated money and ran fundraisers. When Miles first came out as bisexual, she became the GLADD mom and worked with other LGBTQ causes. Her passion was children in need, which likely began when she couldn't have children of her own.

Miles was one of those children she helped. She said when she first heard about him, only a few days old, her heart broke. When she first laid eyes on him, she knew he was meant to be hers.

He would be thankful to his parents every day of his life for adopting him. That didn't mean that sometimes when he

45

looked at them, he didn't wish he could see a little more of himself.

Not so much now, but when he was a kid. He might have grown up in Los Angeles, but there was a time in elementary school when he was one of only three black kids. No child wanted to feel different, yet he almost always had.

"Miles?" his mom asked again, and he frowned, surprised he'd spaced off like that. It must have been hearing Quinn's story earlier, discovering he hadn't been raised by his biological parents either. But unlike Quinn, Miles had a family who loved him. A family he loved. He was grateful as hell for that.

"I'm not working any more than I usually do. I'm not working as much as Dad does. I was out with Ollie, Chance, and Matt last night. I didn't sleep well after that." Because Quinn had asked him to stay…because Quinn had needed him and that was a new experience for him. One that hadn't left his mind since.

She looked over her shoulder at him and smiled. "You boys…I swear. Are you ever going to outgrow your Friday night routine?"

He hoped not. They were among the few people that Miles felt truly at home with. Among the few people he trusted. "Maybe, eventually. But where's the fun in that?" he teased.

"No, I'm glad you still make time to see each other. Friendships are important. You're all lucky to have one another. Vivian says Oliver and Matt are doing well. That they're happy." She turned the water off and began drying the vegetables. Miles's parents were close to Oliver's mom and dad.

Chance's family, as well. Their parents all talked nearly as much as Miles, Oliver, and Chance did.

"Yeah, they're disgustingly happy."

She carried her cutting board and food over to the island.

"Here, let me help." Miles washed his hands and then met her at the center of the large kitchen. She pulled out utensils for him, and the two of them began to chop zucchini and squash.

"There's nothing disgusting about being happy. You'll fall in love at some point as well, even though I doubt you believe it. It might have to be with Chance, since Oliver and Matt are taken, and I'm pretty sure you struggle to let yourself trust anyone other than those three." She cocked a blond brow at him. His mother knew him well. Miles was close to both of his parents, which was why he didn't try to deny it—well, not the trust part. "Chance is like a brother to me, so it looks like I'll just have to stay single."

"You try to pretend you're so growly, but I know my son. Really you're a big softie."

"I'm incredibly growly, I'll have you know," he teased, and she laughed. They had fun together, the two of them. They always had. Where Miles could cook with his mom, laugh with her and talk to her about life, he and his father were both cutthroat attorneys at the same firm and sometimes a little too obsessed with their jobs. Case in point, his father wasn't home at the moment, and it was a Saturday.

If Miles weren't here, he would likely be working as well.

Miles and his mom finished cooking dinner together. Just

as they pulled it out of the oven, his dad came home.

"Sorry I'm late," he said as he made his way into the kitchen. His dad kissed his mom on the cheek and then gave Miles a hug. "Hey, son. I'm glad you came tonight. I wanted to run something by you later. I'm doing some research on a case, and I'd love your opinion."

Miles's chest swelled. It meant a lot to him that his dad cared what he thought, that he asked for Miles's help. He was incredible at what he did, yet he never acted as though he was better than anyone else, and he never hesitated to speak with Miles if he needed a second opinion.

"Of course. No problem."

"Thanks." He gave Miles a kind smile and then ran his hand through his salt and pepper hair. "I'll set the table."

Miles helped his father, and then the three of them sat down to dinner together. They laughed and talked. When they were finished, Miles went into his father's office with him, and they spent a good hour in there as well.

As he drove back to his apartment, his mind shifted to Quinn again. About how light and carefree he was, except for that moment when he'd asked Miles to stay last night and when he'd briefly told Miles what happened. He thought about how different they were...how Quinn was much more open than he was. Then he wondered if there had ever been a time in his life, even if only for a few weeks or months, when he'd felt the same kind of love Miles did from a family. If he'd ever felt like he'd had a family of his own, and for the first time, he wondered why he was the way he was. Why he wanted to be considered *growly* and why he cut himself off from people when he should be spending every day thanking his lucky stars for what he had.

———⁓———

"SHIT," QUINN GROANED as he tested some aspects of a new game they were working on. "Something is up with this level. I don't like the flow of it, but I can't put my finger on what it is."

"See? That's what I thought too. It's too jumpy. Like it doesn't make sense. It's random," his best friend Christian said as they video Skyped. He used to live full time in Los Angeles but moved to Virginia with his boyfriend a while back. His boyfriend was a Motocross racer and spent part of his time in Southern California, and Christian had decided to go back and forth with him.

"Why you always copying me, boo?" Quinn teased him.

Christian rolled his eyes. "Because you're my idol, of course. I want to be just like you, as does everyone else. No one is immune to your superiority."

"Thank fuck you finally admitted it." Quinn leaned back in his chair and put his feet up on the desk. Even though he couldn't be happier for Christian, he missed having his friend here. They'd helped each other through some rough times. If Chris had been here, he wouldn't have embarrassed himself with Miles the other night.

Jesus, he still couldn't believe that.

"You just shook your head. Why did you shake your

head?" Christian asked.

Damn it. "No reason."

"Fuck you. There isn't a chance you would let that go without prying. You should have just said, *I have a headache* or some bullshit excuse like that. Now I know you're hiding something."

"I have a headache," Quinn lied, and they both laughed.

When things settled down, Christian asked, "I'm serious…are you okay? You've seemed a little down lately. Not like the obnoxious Quinn I know and love."

"I resent that. I'm just as obnoxious as I've always been." It was kind of his MO and Quinn was okay with that. People didn't forget him. He made them laugh. That was really all he wanted.

"Are you sleeping okay?" Christian asked, not taking the bait.

Quinn sighed. "I had a little trouble, but then I jerked off into my jersey with your boyfriend's name on it, and that helped."

"I'm serious."

He sighed because he knew Christian *was* serious. He also knew his friend wouldn't let it go until they spoke about it, much like Quinn was with him.

He scratched his head and sighed as he eyed Christian through the computer screen. "I'm good. I promise you, boo. You know me. If I wasn't, I would fly my ass there and squeeze in right between you and your man. I've had a couple of odd nights lately. I'm not sure why, but it prompted me to hook up with this really well-hung top, who fucked me till I passed out, so I can't complain." Or fingered his ass until he did. Honestly, a few days later, he was still a little embarrassed he'd blown his load that quickly.

Christian's brows knitted together in concern. "Are you sure? We can—"

"Yes, I'm sure. Plus, it's only nightmares. It's about time I get over that, anyway. Now can we please talk about you? Or this game you need to figure out because I'm putting this shit on you."

Christian laughed again, but Quinn could tell he didn't feel it. They talked about the game a little more before they ended the Skype.

Quinn rummaged around the office and did a few more things at work before he left the office. Luckily, it was right up the street from his apartment, so he always walked back and forth. On the way, Quinn stopped at Hamburger Mary's and grabbed a quick bite to eat.

When he got back to his place, he fucked around with some graphics on a game he was working on but got bored quickly. He thought about calling a friend to hang out or pull up Grindr, but instead, he found himself typing Miles Sorenson into his search bar.

It popped up with his site and also numerous articles touting his success. He flipped through some of them. "Jesus, baby boy. You're fucking good." Not that he'd had a doubt in his mind that Miles was good at what he did. He was a proud man, that was for sure, and he had this...almost air of superiority about him. Not in a way that made him a dick-head, but like he was one of those people who were just good at everything they did. Like he had success sewn into his DNA, even though Quinn knew he had secrets too.

He clicked on a few of the articles and read about the sexy, bossy top who had him spilling his private life almost as easily as Miles had made him spill his come. The third one spoke about Miles and his father, who was also an attorney. It had a picture of the two men together that unexplainably had his pulse speeding up.

Miles's father was white, and Miles most definitely was not. It wasn't as though that mattered or as if it should have come as a huge shock. One of the things he loved most about Los Angeles was the diversity and how many different families you found here but he would be lying if he didn't admit it made him curious. If it didn't make him wonder about Miles's story. Miles clearly had a family and Quinn never had, but from the first night they spent together, he'd felt a connection with Miles. Like neither of them were as grounded as they wanted people to believe, as they wanted to believe themselves, and maybe this was why.

Quinn, the stalker that he was becoming, exited the page and clicked on the site for his office. From there, he went to the contact page. He thought for a moment. It wasn't likely that Miles checked this email himself, so he would have to be careful in what he said. Part of him figured he shouldn't be messaging at all, but who the hell listened to logic? Quinn didn't.

Mr. Sorenson,

My name is Quinn Barker. We met the other day. You were so kind to offer your expertise, and I feel I shortchanged you. I assure you, this is the first time I haven't gotten the job done. I'd love it if we could talk again. I'll fix my prior error.

Quinn Barker

He added his phone number just in case, submitted the message and wished like hell he could see Miles's face when he got it.

CHAPTER SEVEN

M ILES WAS GOING to kill him.

He read the email from Quinn for the tenth time and smiled. His secretary had sent it through to his private email account earlier that morning and now, every few minutes, he found himself flipping back to it.

At first, he told himself he would ignore it. Eventually, he'd come to terms with the fact that he obviously wasn't doing a good job forgetting about the message, so he just needed to pull his head out of his ass and reply. Unfortunately, he couldn't decide what to say. It was annoying as shit that he was obsessing over it so much in the first place, but he was. Fucker. It was all Quinn's fault. Why couldn't he just leave it alone?

Miles copied the address and composed a new email.

Quinn,

Stalking is illegal, you know. You better not be sitting outside my office right now. This is why I don't give hookups my last name. I'm very familiar with restraining orders and I'm not afraid to use them.

Miles

He hit send and leaned back in his chair. And I'm not afraid to use them? Jesus, that was the corniest shit he'd ever said in his life. What had he been thinking?

Scratch that. Why the fuck did it matter and why was he overthinking stupid emails to some guy he fucked a few times? He wasn't the type to obsess about emails. He realized there was more important shit to worry about than that.

He moved his finger across the mouse to close the tab, just as another message popped up. Miles didn't think twice before clicking it.

Miles,

Is this a private email?

Q

Again, he found himself hitting reply.

Yes.

M

He waited. Jesus, he couldn't believe he sat there watching his damn inbox for a good two minutes before another email popped up.

M,

Does that mean I get to talk dirty to you? Oh! I know. We should have email sex. You like naughty shit. I bet it would feel real forbidden to jerk off at work.

Q

"Oh fuck," Miles mumbled but damned if he didn't have a

smile on his face too. Fucking Quinn. The man seemed to have a knack for making Miles feel less surly, which he didn't understand. Along with the fact that he didn't get why Quinn wasn't surlier than he was.

He checked the time before composing another message.

Sorry. Just finished jerking off. Your timing is off. Again. Now, I have to go to work. Some of us don't get to play with video games all day.

M

The second the message went through, his pulse unexplainably shot up and he found himself typing another message.

That was a joke, by the way. The timing and the video games instead of working.

What the hell was wrong with him? Here he was stressing out over a fucking email to a guy he was never supposed to see again.

Miles pushed to his feet just as he received another message.

I know. You're not quite the bastard you pretend to be.

Q

He stared at the email for far too long. He wasn't even sure why he continued to look or how he would respond. And again, why was he making a big deal out of nothing where Quinn was concerned? It seemed to have become a habit for him.

His eyes darted toward the door when there was a soft knock. "Come in," he called out as his secretary stuck her head in the door. "Did you forget about your meeting, Mr. Sorenson? You're late."

"No, I didn't. Thank you, though. I'm on my way out right now."

But instead, he found himself doing one last thing. He clicked back into the original message from the contact form and added Quinn's number to his phone.

Quinn had him breaking all his rules.

Miles really was going to kill him.

———✦———

IT WAS TUESDAY evening when the first text came through, and Quinn knew right away who it was from. He wasn't sure *how*, but he did and he felt much too excited at the thought of that message.

I can be a bastard, I promise you.

"Holy shit," he whispered. Yes, he'd just been positive this was Miles but seeing it was a different thing. He hadn't heard from Miles since the day before, and then, of course, it had only been email. Miles had taken his number from the contact form and actually sent a fucking message.

Huh.

Stalking is against the law, he replied.

I'm not stalking you. You gave me your phone number. The evidence is on my computer.

He smiled and took a drink of his wine before pausing his

re-watch of *Queer as Folk*.

My mistake, Counselor. To what do I owe the honor of your attention?

Miles replied almost instantly. **Fuck off.**

Fuck me?

I've done that quite a bit, if you remember correctly, Miles replied.

Yeah, I remember. I felt you for days afterward. I had bruises on my hips from your fingers. Bruises he'd fucking loved.

There was a delay in response. After a few minutes, Quinn tossed his cell to the couch, figuring Miles had decided he'd had too much conversation for the day, and was building those walls back up. Quinn fucking hated walls. All they did was cause more damage and hurt more people.

He hit play on his show again but found his eyes kept getting drawn to his cell. It was a few minutes later when it buzzed. He picked it up to see another response from Miles.

You know you liked it.

He grinned. Ah, so they were going to discuss the bruises. **Never said I didn't.**

Somehow Quinn knew this text really was the end of it for tonight. He saved the number in his phone and then went back to watching his show.

He was halfway through his work day on Wednesday, his eyes blurring from all the time he'd spent staring at a computer screen.

He'd been fucking around on this game for months. It wasn't the same one he'd helped Christian test the other day. It wasn't quite as far along in the process, and at the rate it was going, Quinn thought he would blow up the computer rather than have the player in the video game blow things up. He'd always been a fan of blowing, after all.

He rubbed the bridge of his nose, groaned, and then picked up his phone. He considered texting Christian or another friend of his, Michael, but ended up pulling up Miles's phone number instead.

Forest or jungle? he asked.

Is that a real question? Jungle, of course.

Quinn smiled as he looked at the phone. Jungle, huh? Yeah, he could work with that. Before he had the chance to reply, Miles messaged again.

Stop texting me.

You texted me first.

That's because you're a stalker and you looked up my office and emailed me, Miles answered.

Quinn thought for a moment. Wondered why in the fuck he enjoyed this so much, and then typed out his reply. **True. And I'm the one who offered my number, but you're the one who decided you wanted to use it.** And then he turned off his phone, somehow knowing that Miles would drive himself batshit crazy, thinking about what Quinn had just said.

MILES WAS GOING to kill him.

No, it didn't escape his attention that this wasn't the first time he'd thought those words about Quinn this week, but the man was infuriating as fuck.

He'd been the one who showed up at Wild Side last week.

He'd been the one to ask Miles to stay the night.

He'd been the one who emailed him.

He'd been the one to give Miles his phone number and damn it, now Miles was obsessing over the guy. He'd never obsessed over anyone in his life. He fucked and that was it. He worried about his career, his parents, and his friends—that was it—and now he was texting Quinn and getting irritated when Quinn didn't text back and why in the fuck hadn't he texted back, anyway? Was he trying to make Miles lose his mind? If so, it was working.

Still, Miles wasn't the type to chase a man, that was for sure. He'd texted once on Thursday and since Quinn didn't text back, he was over it.

Or he guessed he wasn't over it but he wasn't messaging again.

Who did he think he was? Calling Miles out on using the number Quinn had been the one to give him? Isn't that what you gave people your phone number for?

Holy fucking shit. He was doing it again. If he didn't stop thinking about Quinn he was going to fucking murder someone.

Or murder Quinn. He kept going back to that.

Before Miles drove himself insane or checked into the hospital to see if he'd been given a brain implant he wasn't aware of, Miles went into his bathroom. He opened the glass shower door and turned on the spray. He had dual showerheads. The walls that weren't glass were gray and blue tile, and the floors matched.

It was a ridiculous thing to love, but his shower was one of his favorite things in his apartment.

Miles stripped out of his clothes and stepped under the spray. As he soaped up his balls, he considered rubbing one out real quick. He was slightly sexually frustrated since last weekend. His dick had thought it would get to sink deep inside Quinn's ass again and that obviously hadn't happened and *motherfucker*. Why was he thinking about Quinn again?

He finished cleaning up and got out. He brushed his teeth, thought about shaving but then left the dark stubble along his jaw.

Miles took the towel off his waist as he moved through his bedroom and to his walk-in closet. He let his fingers flick through the shirts hanging there before he again became frustrated with himself and just tugged at the last shirt he'd touched.

It was a white tee with three buttons down the neck, but no collar on it. He paired it with black jeans. Once he was dressed, he grabbed his keys, wallet, and phone and then headed to Wild Side to meet his friends and get his mind off an extremely frustrating and addicting Quinn Barker.

CHAPTER EIGHT

"YOU HAVE AN eyelash on your face." Chance swiped his finger under Miles's eye. When Miles turned and reached for his drink, Chance added, "Wait. Where do you think you're going? Blow." He held his finger out, apparently for Miles to blow the fucking eyelash off. "And you have to make a wish too."

"I'm not making a wish," Miles grumbled. What in the hell did wishes have to do with eyelashes, anyway? It made no damn sense. A lot of what Chance said didn't make sense, though.

"Make a fucking wish, Miles, and stop raining on my parade. You've known me all your life and you know I'm obsessed with wishes. You're extra fucking grumpy tonight, by the way," Chance replied.

Yes, he was being extra fucking grumpy and he knew it, only he didn't know why. "Fine." He blew the lash off Chance's finger.

"What did you wish for?"

"You to leave me alone?"

Oliver chuckled from the other side of him.

"Aww. Come on, baby. You know that's never going to

happen. You don't want it to either." Chance blew a kiss at him, picked up Miles's glass, and finished the rest of the liquid in it. He had a habit of doing that. Miles thought part of the reason was just to annoy people. Chance always got off on that.

"I hate you," Miles told him.

"You love me," Chance replied.

Miles opened his mouth to counter it, but Matt cut him off, "Are you working on a hard case?"

He shrugged, signaled the waitress over, and ordered another drink. "No. Not particularly harder than any other case. I'm just in a bad mood, I guess."

"No! You?" Ollie teased but then winked at him. "And you're not in a bad mood. You're just being Miles, and we love you for it." Sometimes he wondered why they put up with him but he would never tell them that. He would be silently thankful while doing what he could to support them—even if it bothered them while he was doing it.

They all sat around and talked the way they did every Friday night. The longer they stayed the more fidgety he became. Miles never fidgeted. His eyes kept casing the bar. He wouldn't put it past Quinn to show up here just to try and rattle him. He didn't want to let himself think about the fact that it would work, when he'd never been easily shaken before.

The longer they hung out, he started to realize he was actually a bit disappointed Quinn hadn't come. If this had been Ollie thinking about Matt before Matt had gotten his shit together or Chance dreaming about a trick he had, Miles would have been the first one to tell them to chill the fuck out or do something about it. He would also likely come with a list of what could and likely would go wrong because that's just how he rolled.

Thank fuck none of them would do that to him.

"You gonna dance with me or what?" Matt asked Ollie after a few moments of silence. Oliver's eyes lit up. He was so fucking gone for Matt, always had been, but it was good to see Matty looking at Oliver the same way. Miles wasn't looking for what they had, he just wasn't interested, but he was happy for them.

"Of course." The two men got up from the table.

As they left, Chance grabbed Miles's wrist. "Dance with me, Daddy."

Miles rolled his eyes. "I fucking hate it when you call me that."

"Come on. Don't pretend you're not one of those big, top daddies we all love."

He wasn't pretending anything. He knew exactly who and what he was. "Yeah but not with you."

"Nope. Not with me. But we *are* best friends, and I want to dance so it's kind of in your job description to get out there and dance with me."

Which was true. Plus, maybe it would help him get his mind off shit he didn't want his mind on. "Let's go."

They stood up and found an empty spot on the dance floor. Chance wrapped his arms around Miles's shoulders and rode his thigh like he'd done a million times before, as though there was a chance the two of them would go home together.

He put his mouth next to Miles's ear and asked, "You okay?"

Unease skated down Miles's spine. "Yeah, why wouldn't I be?" He went rigid as he waited for Chance to answer.

"Because you just went tense when I asked you that? Because you've been a little off the past week. I can't put my finger on how or why…"

"Oh, sounds like a mystery," Miles teased and Chance laughed.

"It is. And I think you're lying, but I also think you're okay. I'm good at reading people. You know that. So I'm not too worried, but just remember, it's not only okay for you to stick your nose in our business and bust our balls all the time, it's also okay for us to do the same to you."

That wasn't the first time his friends had said something like that to him, and he knew it wouldn't be the last. Miles had no problems talking to them about important things going on in their lives. It was actually really important to him to keep involved and to make sure they were okay…he just didn't like it when the situation was reversed.

"I hear ya," he finally answered.

"Good boy."

"Hey. I'm the one who's supposed to be saying that stuff, remember? I'm the daddy."

They laughed and finished dancing. It wasn't long before the group made their way back to the table. They all ordered another round of drinks except Miles, because the truth was, he knew he would be leaving soon.

He was an answers guy, and he wanted answers about why he had apparently become obsessed with Quinn.

He said his goodbyes to his friends and left early. As soon as he was outside he pulled out his phone and typed out a text.

You home?

The reply came a few seconds later. **Yes.**

I'll be there in ten.

What if I'm busy? Quinn texted back, but Miles turned off his phone without a reply. Two could play at that game.

QUINN KNEW MILES wasn't going to reply to him. Still, he found himself chuckling. "Always have to get the upper hand, you bastard."

It didn't take knowing Miles very long or extremely well to know that.

He sat back down on the couch and picked up the video game controller again. He wasn't going to change his plans because Miles suddenly realized he either wanted to take Quinn up on his offer of another piece of his ass, or because he couldn't handle that Quinn hadn't responded the other day.

It was close to fifteen minutes later when there was a knock at his door. His back was to it, because of the position of the couch. "Come in!" he called out without looking over his shoulder. He continued to slice his way through bad guys on his quest to save his prince.

The door opened, then closed with a soft click. "This is what you're busy doing?" Miles asked in that deep voice that got Quinn's dick hard.

"I had dinner with my friend Tony earlier. I never said I was busy *now*. I just asked, what if I was. Sit down. Check this out."

His character stuck a knife into a man on the screen. Blood shot out, and his character wiped it away from his own face.

"What game is this?" Miles asked as the couch dipped from his weight.

"It's not out yet. I'm doing some final beta testing on it—which means I'm playing it, basically. I'm a mob boss. My boyfriend was kidnapped by a rival crew. I basically kick ass, killing everyone who crosses my path until I get my guy back."

"It's a gay game?" Miles asked, shock apparent in the tone of his voice.

"It gives you the option in the beginning of playing as either a female character or a male. Also, between rescuing your guy or your girl. I thought of it myself." He nudged Miles's arm playfully. "We need more options like that."

"This is yours? You did this?" Miles rested his elbows on his knees and leaned in, looking much more interested than he had a moment ago. His white shirt stretched across his arms, and Quinn considered dropping the controller and sitting on his dick, but he didn't.

"I did. I'm kind of a big deal."

A loud laugh jumped out of Miles's mouth. It sounded good on him.

"Big deal my ass."

"You mean my ass? My ass is a big deal? I know." Quinn

clicked a few buttons and backtracked. "Oh fuck. You made me mess up."

"I made you mess up? What did I do?"

Quinn got shot, but yeah, of course he managed to survive it for his next life. He held the controller out for Miles. "Do you want to try?"

His eyes darted to the controller then at Quinn's face. He could see the...hell, what almost looked like confusion there. Like he hadn't expected Quinn to ask or he didn't want to let himself say yes, or as though he didn't understand the question. But then he reached out. His finger brushed Quinn's hand as he took the remote from him...and started to play.

He died right away of course. He cursed and then said, "Fuck that. I'm going again."

Quinn laughed. "Obviously, you can't let a video game get the best of you."

"It didn't get the best of me. I just need to figure out what in the fuck I'm doing."

Quinn explained the controls to him, and Miles played again...and again. He watched as Quinn took a turn. Took another one himself.

When it was Quinn's play again, Miles grabbed his arm as Quinn tried to make his way through an abandoned building. "No! What are you doing? Don't go that way. What the fuck? I saw something behind you. Why aren't you listening to me?"

"Oh, so you even know better on a game I made? Let the professional handle this."

"Professional my ass. You're going to get us killed again

and then I'm going to have to *spank* your ass."

Quinn risked a glance at him. "Oh, so I should die on purpose, then?"

Miles ignored him. He flopped back on the couch. "Oh my fucking God. I can't believe you're not listening to me. Give me the controller before I take it from you. Let me handle this."

Okay…so apparently Miles liked control in all aspects of his life, and not just the bedroom. And he apparently now liked video games more than sex, too. Quinn didn't mind the first part so much, but they were going to have to figure something out about the video-game-over-sex thing.

When Quinn died again, he passed the controller to Miles without a word. He turned and watched as Miles lost himself in the game and Quinn got to study him.

The way his shirt stretched across his arms and chest. The outline of his hard, dark nipples against the white fabric. His hands were strong and veiny. His eyes a whiskey brown. His tongue snuck out every once in a while and traced his lips. He had a strong jawline, dark lashes. Jesus, he was hot as hell.

Why were they playing video games again?

As though he felt Quinn's eyes on him, Miles glanced at him. "What?" he asked.

"Nothing." Because there was nothing really to say. This was a new side of Miles, and he enjoyed it.

"I can't believe you did this." Miles didn't look at him, just kept playing, his eyes locked on the screen.

"Why not?"

"I don't know…it's cool, though. That you had a hand in this from beginning to end. I don't think I really got it when you told me what you do."

"Most people don't. It would be even different if you saw the creation stage. I guess it's just like any job. If you don't do it, you don't get it. I mean, you're a fucking lawyer. That's a whole lot more incredible than making a video game."

Miles didn't look at him. Quinn thought maybe it was easier on him if he didn't. "Just incredible in different ways," he replied. Then he died, dropped the controller on his lap, and rested his head against the couch. "I'm done…what time is it?"

"After two."

His eyes went wide and yeah, Quinn was surprised as well. They'd been at it for over three hours.

They were both silent for a moment. Quinn leaned against the back of the couch like Miles was. Both of them had their feet on the coffee table as they stared at the TV screen.

"Can I ask you something?" Miles said, his voice quiet, almost a low growl that said he didn't want to ask whatever his question was.

"You can ask me anything." Because mostly, Quinn was an open book. At least when he trusted someone, and for whatever reason, he trusted Miles.

"Did you ever know your parents? What happened to them?"

His brows pulled together because he hadn't expected Miles to ask him that. Hadn't expected it to still be on his mind. "No one knows who my father was. My mom never said. She didn't have any family, at least not that we know of. She was young…poor. She passed away when I was five. A few of her friends wanted to take me but they couldn't. Most of them were just like her—young, no education, and hardly enough money to make ends meet, so I got put into the system. Some of them tried to keep in touch with me, but you know how that shit goes. Eventually, we lost contact."

"You were young."

Out of the corner of his eye, Quinn saw movement. He turned to see that Miles had rolled his head so he was looking Quinn's way. "I was."

"You weren't adopted, though?"

He gave a soft chuckle even though there was nothing funny about the situation. "I wasn't really the kind of kid most people were looking for… I was angry at the world for a long time. I got into trouble and I wouldn't speak to anyone and…well, I wasn't very nice to them either. I hated all the mothers I met because they were alive, and mine wasn't. I hated siblings in the houses I would go to because they had parents, and I didn't. I hated them because they wouldn't let me be with my mother's friends. I ran away, said hurtful things. I wasn't the absolute joy to be around that I am now."

Quinn hoped Miles would laugh, but he didn't. He just looked…sad. Confused. Quinn wasn't sure where the confusion came from.

"I can't imagine you being angry or hurtful to anyone. You're not anymore."

No…no he wasn't. He'd gotten tired of pushing people away. "It wasn't a fun way to live." And he'd seen what anger could do to a person. Seen how the way you treated others could come back at you. "Why are you so interested in my past, Counselor? You fall in love with me? We talked about this in the beginning."

Quinn finally got a small chuckle out of Miles, but it didn't last long. Miles took a deep breath…then another one. He wrung his fingers together before stopping suddenly, as though he saw that as a sign of weakness. He sat up a little straighter and said, "I was left in an alley at a couple days old. Someone took out their trash and they heard me crying. They realized someone had thrown me away."

Oh fuck… Quinn's heart sped up. A thick, heavy rolling sensation worked its way through his gut.

"I had drugs in my system, was malnourished. I almost died, obviously, I didn't. I'm here and everything is fine." He shifted his position nervously. "Fuck, I've never told anyone that story before. I think it's time I go."

Miles stood, and when Quinn did as well, his legs nearly gave out. It was like his bones had gone soft and could hardly hold him up. "Don't go," he said, but Miles already had his back to him and was heading for the door.

"I need to."

This was their connection, Quinn realized. It was the piece that tied them together. The draw he'd felt to Miles and one he believed Miles had felt to him. Though there were different circumstances, they'd both grown up without their biological parents. They'd both been in the system somehow, both been at someone else's mercy.

"Miles," Quinn said and the other man stopped at the door.

When Quinn reached him, he put his hands at Miles's hips. Leaned his forehead against Miles's back. Slowly, Quinn's hands slid forward until they wrapped around Miles's waist.

They were that way one beat, then two and three, and before he knew it, Miles turned on him. Took control as he grabbed Quinn, pushed him against the wall, heavy pressure from his fingertips digging into Quinn's skin. And then Miles's mouth collided with his.

It was a kiss filled with hunger, with anger, and maybe some pain too. It was Miles putting things back on his terms. Taking control and Quinn gladly giving it up to him.

Their teeth clanked against each other's. Miles's cock pressed against Quinn's. He bit at Quinn's lip and sucked his tongue, and in this moment, Quinn would gladly let Miles overpower him in any way he wanted.

But just as quickly as it started, Miles jerked away. Quinn expected him to immediately walk out. To cut contact because this was becoming something totally different from what it was supposed to be. But then…it had been that way their first weekend, hadn't it? If not, they would have fucked and Miles would have been gone an hour later.

Miles's breath was hot against Quinn's face, and he knew the other man was trying to hold himself back.

When he stepped away slowly, he said, "Thank you."

"What are you thanking me for?" Quinn asked.

"I don't know." And then, he walked out of the apartment, and Quinn tried to figure out what in the hell was going on.

CHAPTER NINE

The Weekend

"*T*HAT WAS FUN. *You're good with your dick.*" *Quinn fell back on his bed, panting. They were both covered in sweat. Miles's chest rose and fell with the same short, sharp intakes and releases as Quinn's did.*

"*Only good?*" *he found himself asking. "I need to step up my game.*"

Quinn rolled over and looked at him. "Oh, did I use the wrong words? Does someone need their ego stroked? Okay, how about fantastic? Magnificent? Awe-inspiring. The best lay I've ever had?"

Miles rolled his eyes and playfully pushed a pillow into Quinn's face. The movement took him by surprise. It was…comfortable. And not comfortable in his sexual prowess kind of way, but…familiar, he guessed. As though he and Quinn knew one another better than they did or had a real relationship outside of a random hookup. It was really fucking weird.

Still, he kept it going. "You're getting closer. Still not good enough, though."

"*My opinion matters that much to you, huh?*" *Quinn winked at him, and Miles didn't like the direction this was going.*

"Nah. I know I'm good."

"What? I thought you were fantastic? Magnificent? Awe-inspiring?"

Damn it. The bastard always seemed to one-up him. Just as Miles was about to reply, Quinn's stomach growled loudly enough for Miles to hear it.

"Are you a little hungry there?" Miles asked.

"Are you going to feed me?"

"My cock," he teased.

"Real food, then dick. Let's go. If you're not going to feed me, I'll have to feed us both."

He rolled out of the bed without waiting for Miles. Quinn walked naked to the door, and Miles thought this would be a good time for him to bow out. To end this…whatever the fuck it was and go home. They'd both come more than once, so really, there was no point in staying.

Quinn made it all the way to the door before he stopped, turned, and looked at Miles. His dick was soft, between his legs. His stomach flat and sexy, and that damn grin on his face that he always had. Was the guy ever not smiling?

When his lips stretched even farther, Miles saw his sexy little dimples that he wanted to lick.

"Are you coming or what?" Quinn asked.

No. It was time to go home. "Hopefully soon. Eat first, fuck later, remember?" he said and then pushed out of Quinn's bed. Wrong answer. He'd just given the wrong answer, but he didn't care.

Still naked, they walked into Quinn's kitchen. He didn't have much to eat, so they threw a frozen pizza into the oven.

"What do you do?" Quinn asked as their food baked.

"Lawyer," Miles admitted. It wasn't typically a topic of conversation when he hooked up but none of this was standard.

"That doesn't surprise me."

"Oh no?" he asked.

"I bet you're good at it too. I think you're likely good at everything you do. Or magnificent, I should say. You're a perfectionist because it's easier to be perfect than to fuck with emotional stuff."

Quinn was absolutely right about that. Miles also didn't want to get into that. "And you're good at psychoanalyzing me. Since I'm not paying you for it, don't bother." He walked over to Quinn, backed him up against the fridge.

Their bodies touched, and Miles instantly started to get hard again.

"Kiss me," he told Quinn.

Just like that, Quinn leaned in. He traced Miles's lips with his tongue, pushed his way inside and Miles let him. He thrust his cock against Quinn's, held his hips tightly, and slowly made out with him.

When he let his mouth trail down Quinn's throat, he mumbled, "You're magnificent at kissing too."

Miles smiled against Quinn's neck.

When the timer went off, signaling the pizza was ready, Miles pulled away. Kissing had been the perfect distraction. "I'll get it."

"I'll let you. Just don't burn your dick off, okay? I'm not done with it yet."

Miles laughed again. Goddamn him.

SWEAT DRIPPED DOWN Miles's head as he ran on his treadmill. When it stung his eyes, he wiped them with a towel that hung on the machine but didn't slow his pace.

He had a whole lot of shit to figure out.

One of the things he prided himself on was the fact that he was no-nonsense. He didn't bullshit, and he was honest, which didn't count for a whole lot if he wasn't honest with himself.

There was a part of him that liked Quinn.

Or thought he *could* like Quinn.

Or felt some kind of connection to him that he didn't have with Chance, Matt, and Ollie. Not just sexually, either.

It was one of the three of those things. Maybe a combination. Or all of them. He hadn't quite figured it all out yet, but he wasn't going to lie to himself about it.

Admitting it didn't mean he liked this new bit of truth because he wasn't really fond of putting himself out there, but it was a truth all the same.

Sweat stung his eyes again, and after wiping his face, Miles slowed the pace of the treadmill.

Last night, he'd told Quinn about being left. About being abandoned.

It wasn't as though no one knew. Chance, Matt, and Ollie obviously did, because their families were close and they'd grown up together. One look at his parents showed he hadn't been born to them, but the story wasn't something he or his parents offered to many. Miles had never wanted sympathy for his beginning and his parents had never wanted praise for taking a baby who had been thrown away. It was his story to tell, he just never thought it was anyone's business...yet he'd told Quinn.

The bastard.

If he hadn't just admitted he'd liked the guy, he'd hate him.

Why had it been Quinn he picked up in the bar that night? Why had he not only been an incredible fuck, but also charming and funny and completely annoying, which Miles also strangely found endearing?

Oh God... Miles was obsessed with him. He'd become Ollie with Matt, only Miles obviously wasn't in love since he hardly knew the guy.

He didn't like feeling uncertain and Quinn made him feel that way.

Again—the bastard.

If Ollie could see him now, he'd have a field day with this shit.

Miles stopped the treadmill and got off. He really needed to do something to get his mind off of Quinn, but he sure as shit couldn't call Oliver. He had this fear that Ollie would somehow see right through him.

Matt...they were close friends, but they'd never been the type who hung out without Ollie and Chance, so that wouldn't make sense. Chance was actually the perfect one of his friends to choose anyway, but he knew Chance had a dancing gig today.

There was no one else he trusted besides the three of

them…well, except suddenly the very man who had him all tied up.

He picked up his phone and stabbed at the screen as though his cell was what had him so pissed off.

"Miss me already?" Quinn said instead of hello, and even though Miles wanted to scowl, he couldn't.

"Come over."

"No," Quinn answered.

Oh…well he hadn't expected that. "Why not?"

"Hmm," Quinn said. "Maybe because you didn't ask nice-ly."

Oh for fuck's sake. "Will you please come over, Quinn? How was that?" He really, really was going to kill the man.

"Better…but I still can't come."

"What? Why?"

"Because this is moving too fast for me…"

Miles's pulse unexpectedly sped up. Moving too fast for him? What did he think Miles wanted from him?

"You want me to see your apartment? Isn't that against some super secret, *hookup* code you have? And what about me? What if I have a super secret, hookup code you don't know about? Huh? What about that?"

"I…" And then, damn it, he started to laugh. Why did Quinn make him laugh so damn much? "Get your ass over here. We need to talk."

Quinn gave an exaggerated sigh. "Fine, but only because you're pretty and bossy and I have a thing for pretty and bossy. What's your address?"

Miles gave it to him and they ended the call.

He only wore a pair of shorts and nothing else. He thought about taking a shower but knew it wouldn't take Quinn very long to get here, so instead he went into the kitchen and poured himself some bourbon, because who didn't want alcohol at one in the afternoon?

Glass in hand, Miles walked over to the nearly floor-to-ceiling window that overlooked the city.

He took a sip of his drink, watched the cars below—the sky that went on forever and the bright Southern California sun—and realized he was tired. Tired of feeling so trapped inside of himself. Of the fear he never really understood but had always felt.

When he looked at Quinn, he didn't see the same hesitation he had and Miles realized for the first time, that he wished he were more like that. More carefree and easy-going and not so damn bottled up.

He just didn't know what to do about it.

It was a few minutes later when his bell rang.

Miles waited a moment, draining the rest of his bourbon before he turned and walked for the door. On the way, he set his glass on the bar.

As soon as he opened the door, Quinn cocked a brow at him. "This is getting out of hand—all this time we've spent together. One would think we like each other…or at least that we want to know each other. We weren't supposed to want to know each other, were we?"

"No, we weren't," Miles answered honestly. "Though I

think that was likely more me than it was you."

"I think it was, too." Quinn stepped inside. Miles closed the door. Quinn looked around his apartment, and he tried to figure out what he saw when he looked at it.

It was decorated nicely—all modern, stainless steel appliances. Lots of gray, which was his favorite color. He had some steel artwork and a few blues thrown in, but that was the extent of it.

"Wow...is it me or is it frosty in here? And I'm a little afraid to touch anything. This looks like a real adult's apartment to me. Is it kid-proofed?"

"It probably needs to be kid-proofed if you're going to be here," Miles teased, as a smile tugged at the corners of his lips, and his chest got a strange lightness.

Quinn had a similar playfulness that Chance had, yet different at the same time. He'd never wanted Chance the way he consistently wanted his dick inside Quinn. Even when he fought himself on it.

"And wait...what do you mean by frosty?"

"It's cold, Miles, and I don't mean the temperature, but it fits you too."

The two of them made their way toward Miles's couch. "Cold fits me? Fuck you very much."

"Don't worry. I still like you." Quinn winked at him. "And I know it's mostly an act."

People really needed to quit saying that to him. "It's not an act."

"Whatever you say, Counselor."

Miles pointed to the couch and said, "Sit."

"Woof!" His eyes went wide at Quinn's bark. Still, he sat down. "Do I at least get a treat for being a good boy? I really like bones."

Just like that, his cock started to swell. He'd rather fuck Quinn and forget the rest of it, but damn it, if he didn't get some answers he was going to drive himself crazy. "We'll see if you earn my bone."

Quinn leaned back on the couch and crossed his arms. Miles knew he wasn't going to say anything. That he would sit there and wait until Miles got out whatever he needed to get out, and he was partially thankful for it but also annoyed. He didn't want to feel like he could read Quinn and he sure as shit didn't want Quinn to be able to read him.

"You're driving me out of my fucking mind." Miles ran a hand over his head as he started to pace the room.

"Me? What did I do?"

"I don't fucking know and that's the thing that's driving me batshit crazy. I don't like not having the answers, Quinn. One plus one is always two. It's always been two for me, but now there are all these fucking variables that make me continuously come up with a different answer." He had no idea if what he was saying made any sense. It did in his head, but by the way Quinn's brows knitted together, he was pretty sure Quinn had reduced him to speaking gibberish.

"Me spending the weekend with you? That was not one plus one equaling two. Me coming home with you from Wild Side and staying when you asked? Nope. Not two either. Asking about your past sure as hell wasn't two and texting and emailing isn't two and playing video games and telling you about my past is as far from fucking two as you can get."

"So, I'm kind of like the anti-two?" Quinn asked and Miles stopped moving. He turned and looked at him and, mother-fucker, he wanted to kiss him. Wanted to shove Quinn to his knees and force his cock into Quinn's mouth and fuck it.

"You're ridiculous."

"But you're also smiling…and looking at me like you want to jump my bones. Looks like I might earn my treat after all."

He wanted to laugh. Damn it all to hell, he wanted to fucking laugh but this was serious to him. Miles needed to understand what was going on.

"Why aren't you two?" he asked, hating the vulnerability in his voice. He'd never been vulnerable to anyone in his life, outside of Chance and Oliver.

Quinn sighed. "Maybe I *am* two. Maybe I'm not. Maybe I'm just a really good fuck or maybe you realize you're tired of keeping yourself closed off or maybe we're destined to be best friends. Maybe we'll just screw each other's brains out for a few weeks and then never see each other again, and that's the way it's supposed to be. You can't always have the answers."

"But I need them," he said simply, because it was true. If he were a shrink, he'd say it was because he didn't have answers about his own past. Because he didn't know where he'd come from besides that trash can in an alley. And because of that, he needed answers. He needed things to make sense and he also needed to protect himself. That's what he tried to ingrain into Ollie for years when it came to Matt. He needed to protect himself, so he didn't get hurt. So he didn't get left.

But he wasn't a shrink so he wasn't saying all of that.

Quinn stood and walked over to him. He stopped right in front of Miles. "The first weekend you stayed because we were both lonely and we're good in bed together. You spent the night after Wild Side because you're a good man and you knew I couldn't be alone. The shit after that? Who knows. Like I said, maybe it's the sex. Or it could be that we have shit in common you don't have with anyone else. Because I know what it's like to wonder...*what if* and to have no one around you connected by blood. Or it could just be because I'm fucking adorable, addicting, and a blast to be around. The only way to know is not to fight it and to see how things go. You're not going to find the answers to this one in a law book, Miles. You either have to walk away or explore it and see what happens."

He reached out and touched Miles's chest. Quinn's pale fingers were such a sharp contrast to his darker skin. Quinn's thumb brushed against his nipple and, motherfucker, it made Miles shudder.

"So what's it going to be, Counselor? Do I have to go, or did I earn a reward?"

His heart sped up and a low growl vibrated through his chest. He was going to do this. Fuck, he was really going to do this. Miles was going to see what could happen between himself and Quinn...he wanted to. "You know you were a good boy. Go to my room. Last door on the right, and I'll give you what you want."

Damned if it wasn't what he wanted too.

CHAPTER TEN

Q UINN FELT LIKE he was drunk. His body was buzzing and his pulse flying. He was on a high being fed by his lust. By desire for the pleasure he knew Miles would give him.

And maybe, just maybe, because he'd held his breath waiting for Miles to say yes. Because he felt the connection tying them together and he wanted to explore it as well.

"Hurry your ass up!" he called as he sped down the hallway.

Just as Quinn was about to turn into the bedroom, Miles grabbed his waist from behind, stopping him. "You seem to have forgotten I call the shots." He stopped and pulled Quinn back so his ass was tucked against a hard cock. Miles bent forward, bit Quinn's earlobe then sucked it. Quinn's bones damn near melted right then and there.

"You seem to have forgotten, no matter how much I like that, I also enjoy testing your patience, too."

Miles chuckled in his ear. "Oh, I remember." His palm skated around Quinn's hip until he squeezed Quinn's cock. A shudder rocked through him that he could tell vibrated through Miles as well.

Quinn inhaled, smelled the soft scent of sweat on Miles's

skin. Had he been working out before he practically demanded Quinn came over? He was certainly dressed like he had been.

"You're trembling you're so damn hungry for my cock, aren't you?" Miles whispered against his ear.

Yeah…yeah he was. Quinn had always loved sex. Who didn't? There was nothing, nothing he liked more than being fucked, more than the feel of a man filling him. The fact that he knew what Miles could do? That he knew Miles could drive him so fucking crazy it felt like an out of body experience? That just made the need ricocheting around inside him even more intense. Like he would lose his fucking mind if Miles didn't hurry up and take him.

"Are you going to give it to me? If not I can go…" Quinn pretended to try and pull out of Miles's grasp, but his fingers just dug deeper into Quinn's hip and the hand on his erection squeezed tighter.

"You don't get to leave now. You already got me intrigued by you so now you have to stay until I've had my fill."

Which was fucking fine with Quinn. Actually, it was more than fine, but he wouldn't inflate Miles's head any more than it already was by telling him.

"Go," Miles said in his ear while he swatted his ass. The sting he loved rushed through him, welcome and exciting. Quinn walked to the bathroom connected to Miles's room, hoping for more where that came from, with Miles on his heels. The room was huge, filled with more grays like the living room, his shower, big enough for a large orgy.

"Throw many parties in here?" Quinn teased as he stepped

out of his shoes. Miles didn't answer. He pinned Quinn with his stare that was all fire and want and dominance and confusion.

He almost called Miles out on it. Told Miles he was just as fucking hungry for Quinn's ass as Quinn was for cock, but the little voice of reason in the back of his mind which he rarely listened to told him he shouldn't.

So, instead he pulled his shirt over his head, as Miles watched.

He pulled his pants and underwear off, saw Miles's breathing speed up.

"You gonna stand there all day, or you gonna give me what I want?" He wanted his scalp to sting from Miles pulling his hair. His ass to burn from the other man's hand. He wanted his lips swollen from kissing and his hole filled and stretched until he wasn't sure he could take any more.

Again, Miles stayed silent. He walked over to the shower and turned it on. Tested the temperature for a moment. Quinn watched his muscular back as he did so, wanted his tongue to lick a path down all that dark, salty skin.

It was a quick moment later that Miles told him, "Come here," and Quinn did. He stopped right in front of the man, who then said, "Let me see it."

Quinn knew exactly what he was talking about. He turned, giving Miles his ass. He traced a finger down Quinn's crack and damned if he didn't nearly melt again.

He palmed Quinn's ass cheeks as he said, "Jesus, this ass. I want to tear it up."

Quinn's cock ached, he was so fucking hard. He leaked all over the damn floor. "Then do it, Counselor."

Miles turned him, took his mouth in a bruising kiss. His tongue pushed into Quinn's mouth as his finger nudged its way between Quinn's cheeks. He rubbed Quinn's hole, and he immediately widened his stance to give Miles better access. They kissed, Miles petting Quinn's rim until he nearly lost his mind. Christ, he loved having his ass teased and played with.

He licked Miles's neck, tasted the salt there. He moaned and licked again, and Miles growled in response.

Finally, after what felt like an eternity, Miles shoved his shorts down. Quinn watched his thick cock burst free and wanted his lips stretched around the fat rod. Wanted Miles to push Quinn's face into his pubes. Wanted the rough hairs to scratch against his face and the masculine scent of Miles to fill his nostrils.

He wanted to go crazy.

He wanted to drive Miles there too.

Quinn knew how good he was at worshiping a dick and knew firsthand what his mouth did to Miles.

"Want me on my knees?" Quinn asked.

"Maybe," Miles answered and then, "Get in the shower."

They both climbed inside. Miles stepped under the spray, water pouring down his muscular body. "You are so fucking sexy," Quinn told him and earned himself one of Miles's grins.

"You're not so bad yourself."

"Not so bad? I'm fucking fierce, thank you very much," he teased.

"Wash me," Miles told him, and Quinn picked up the liquid soap and a sponge. He squirted some of the soap onto the black material and ran it over Miles's body—his chest, shoulders, under the arms he wanted to bury his face in, before traveling lower, to his stomach, and then down more until he reached his cock.

Miles groaned when Quinn soaped his balls. When he stroked his dick with a slick hand.

Jesus, he was big—heavy sac, thick cock with veins Quinn wanted to lick.

"That's enough, baby boy," Miles said, a rough edge to his voice that rubbed Quinn the right way. "I'm going to be the one shooting too soon this time."

"Don't ever mention that again. I have a reputation to protect."

Miles gave him a half grin. "You'll make up for it." He stepped under the spray again and rinsed himself. Once the soap was gone, he backed up away from the showerhead and nodded toward the floor. "Get on your knees for me now. I want your mouth."

He gave Quinn one more bruising kiss and then pushed him down. Quinn went easily. He'd always loved this, being more submissive when he fucked. He didn't like to be told what to do in his everyday life, but here? When he was with a man? He fucking reveled in it.

When he settled himself and looked up at Miles, he grabbed the base of his erection and asked, "You want it?"

"You know I do," Quinn replied.

"Then take it."

Quinn did just that. He licked a straight line from the base of Miles's cock to the head. Let his tongue circle the crown before he made his way back down again.

He nuzzled Miles's sac, smelled the fresh soap on his skin, and savored the feel of his rough pubes against his cheek.

It wasn't until he opened wide, stretched his lips around the erection in front of him to take Miles deep, that he was treated with the stinging of his scalp as Miles fisted his hair. He knotted his hand in it until Quinn shuddered.

His own cock was so damn hard, he worried he'd embarrass himself again. That if he lowered his hand and wrapped it around himself, it would only take a few strokes before he shot himself all over the floor of Miles's shower. He concentrated on the job at hand, at sucking Miles, at swallowing as much of him as he could because if there was ever a dick that deserved to be worshiped, it was this one.

"Christ, that fucking mouth of yours drives me so crazy. Such a smart, sarcastic mouth until it's full of dick."

Quinn's eyes rolled back. Those words made what he was doing even better.

He continued working Miles's cock. Wanted attention on his own, on his hole that would soon get what Miles was so good at giving.

There was a sharp pull to his hair, strong enough to tilt Quinn's head up. The tip of Miles's cock was at his lips. He knew Miles would pull back soon so he kissed the end before he was jerked to his feet.

Miles still held him by the back of the head. Their lips were inches apart now, breaths heavy, Miles panting as he looked at Quinn.

He breathed in, Miles out, Miles in, Quinn out.

"You gonna fuck me or what, Counselor?" he finally asked, and then they were stumbling out of the shower—teeth clanking, tongues slashing, lips searching.

He felt like Miles was going to devour him, take him whole, and in this moment, he would welcome it.

Miles kissed him until they got to the sink. "Bend over it," he said, and goose bumps shot across Quinn's skin at the command.

He did as Miles said. Miles's hand brushed down his back, his finger tracing each rise and fall of Quinn's spine. "Perfect arch."

Quinn looked up, met Miles's eyes in the mirror and replied, "I know." Because he did. He was fucking good at this.

"Mouthy little bottom, aren't you?" Miles teased.

"Realistically confident."

"You're killing me." Miles looked away, and Quinn knew it was because this was a lot. Because just fucking before he'd admitted that Quinn intrigued him was one thing, but now they both knew this was about more than just a piece of ass. What? They hadn't gotten that far yet and didn't know each other well enough to figure it out either, but it was a truth between them that hadn't been there the first weekend they'd shared.

Or maybe they had known it but hadn't been able to admit

it.

"Get in me," Quinn told him.

"Mouthy," Miles said again. "Going to have to do something about that." He winked at Quinn in the mirror before he rummaged in the drawer next to him. He pulled out a condom, ripped it with his teeth, and sheathed that big dick that Quinn couldn't wait to feel.

There was lube on the counter, and Quinn almost commented on it, but then Miles was squirting his fingers and, fuck…his eyes rolled back as Miles rubbed his hole.

He pushed his finger in and fucked Quinn with it. "Remember what happened last time you did that," Quinn said between fast breaths. "I came too soon."

"I remember," Miles replied. "Don't do it again." He didn't stop, pushed another finger inside. Quinn's balls were begging to let loose. Just when he thought he couldn't take it anymore, Miles lubed his cock, leaned closer, and pushed the fat head past Quinn's rim.

"Oh God." His eyes fluttered. He loved this, loved being stretched by a thick cock.

And it was a stretch. Miles slowly worked his way inside Quinn. Each delicious inch almost made Quinn lose his head, but then Miles was buried to the hilt and his fingers dug into Quinn's hips and their eyes met in the mirror.

"Give it to me," Quinn told him, and Miles did.

He pulled almost all the way out and slammed forward again, railed into him with everything he had. They watched each other in the mirror. He watched Miles's muscles flex and veins spring to life in his neck and wondered what was sweat and what was water from the shower.

He held Quinn's hips tighter. There would be bruises and Quinn would love them. His body jerked forward every time Miles slammed into him from behind.

Quinn reached up, tried to grab the edge of the counter and knocked over anything in his way.

Miles just smiled and kept fucking and Quinn held on for dear life.

Every time Miles pushed in, he hit Quinn's prostate just right.

When Miles leaned over him—his chest to Quinn's back, pushing his hips into the edge of the counter, and pressed a kiss to Quinn's temple—he fucking lost it. His balls let go and he shot all over—once, twice, three fucking times before Miles's teeth teased his shoulder, then bit gently as he shuddered and groaned and came right along with Quinn.

They lay there, the shower still going, shaving cream and a toothbrush container knocked over, looking at each other in the mirror, both of them likely wondering what in the fuck was going on.

Just as Miles went to pull away, Quinn mumbled, *"Fantastic, magnificent,"* and earned a smile from Miles in return.

CHAPTER ELEVEN

QUINN WAS PASSED out beside him, with his leg bent, and his knee against Miles. His cock was soft, resting in neatly trimmed, dark pubic hair. He had four bruises on each hip from where Miles had held on to him. His skin was pale—pale enough that Miles figured he needed to tease him about getting some sun. His mouth was slightly open as he breathed. His jawline brushed with stubble, and just looking at him, Miles could feel his cock begin to stir. He wanted to roll Quinn over, spread his ass cheeks and push his dick inside Quinn's addicting little hole.

But he didn't do that. Instead, he watched Quinn nap as he replayed their morning—the confusing vulnerability he had with this man. The connection he'd maybe created in his own fucking brain because there were millions of people in the world who'd been abandoned or been in foster care or adopted.

"Mmm. I'm hungry. Do you cook? I don't cook. We can *not cook* together." The weekend they'd spent together, Quinn had been low on any kind of food that didn't go in the microwave or wasn't a frozen meal, so they hadn't gotten far enough to know if either one of them really cooked.

Quinn rolled over. Miles had his hand locked behind his head with his elbows bent, and Quinn nuzzled himself inside Miles's armpit.

Miles rolled his eyes. "How do we eat if we *not cook* together?"

"Not cooking means cooking but doing it badly." He found his way out of Miles's arm, looked at him, and winked. "Pay attention, Counselor. It's not that hard to keep up."

Oh for fuck's sake. "When you speak gibberish, it is. How in the hell was I supposed to know what *not cooking* is? How about we order out? Or throw something easy in the oven? That feels a whole lot easier than doing something neither of us are good at."

Quinn's smile turned into a frown. "Oh, does Mr. Perfect not like doing things he's not good at?"

What kind of question was that? "Does anyone like doing things they're not good at?"

"Yes, yes they do, Miles. That's how you *get* good at things…or you're just shitty at it forever and that's okay because you can't be good at everything."

"Yes, yes I can, Quinn." Miles spoke the same way Quinn had spoken to him and then slipped out from under him and walked over to his dresser.

As he pulled on a pair of black boxer briefs, Quinn said, "You have a nice ass. Do you ever bottom?"

Miles stopped, looked at him. Huh. He hadn't expected that question. Quinn definitely loved bottoming. "I have. I will. If I'm being honest, I strongly prefer to top though. Is topping me something you're interested in?"

Quinn didn't move, just continued to lie on the bed watching him. "First, I don't think you're ever anything except honest, so no need to preface anything you say with that. Second, at this time? No. You know I like dick in my ass, but I was just curious if it was a preference or just a control thing with you. Actually, it might be exhausting to top you. I'm sure you're a bossy bottom."

Miles chuckled. "Me? Whatever gave you that idea?"

"Oh, let me think. I don't know. What could ever give me that idea?" Quinn stood, stretched, then scratched his balls.

"Do you have an itch you'd like me to scratch?"

Quinn began to walk toward the bathroom. "Nah. It was a little boring last time."

"You little fucker." Miles wrapped his hand around Quinn's wrist and jerked Quinn toward him.

Quinn playfully tried to fight him, but Miles overpowered him easily. He maneuvered Quinn against the wall, held him there with his body, and buried his face in Quinn's neck, sucking on the skin there. He felt Quinn go lax immediately and found himself smiling. "Boring, huh? Is that why you tremble every time I touch you? Is that why you damn near come out of your skin every time I'm inside of you?" He rutted against Quinn again.

"Okay...so maybe I exaggerated a little."

"A lot," Miles said and then sucked Quinn's earlobe. "Tell me I drive you crazy..."

"Well, you *are* annoying as hell so..." Quinn said breathlessly, making Miles smile into his neck. Damn it. The man could always make him smile.

"Tell me. I drive. You crazy," he said again. "Tell me you're always hungry for my cock."

"Only if you say the same thing about me."

"Well, you *are* annoying as hell..." Miles tried to use Quinn's words on him.

"See? That's what I thought. If you can't admit it, I won't admit it. I think I'm going to make it my mission to ensure you don't always get your way. I think you're likely too used to getting it."

Miles's hold on Quinn eased up, and that's when he took advantage and slipped around him.

"This is going to be fun! I'm so glad we decided to see where this goes. I'm going to enjoy turning you inside out, Miles Sorenson."

Quinn walked into the bathroom, leaving Miles standing there, unstable on his own feet. No one had ever made him feel unsteady before, yet he had a feeling Quinn would constantly put him in that state.

He was so fucked.

QUINN HAD BORROWED a pair of sweats from Miles, and then they'd ordered Chinese food. It had just arrived a moment before. Miles headed straight for the table, but Quinn said, "No. I don't think so. Let's eat on the patio. I need some color."

He was surprised when Miles cocked a brow at him and said, "Yeah, I was noticing that in bed earlier."

Fucker. "I meant because your apartment is so gray, but I think you know that. And I burn, thank you very much."

He liked this, though. Enjoyed the laughter and the fun from Miles. He was hard to nail down, in a lot of ways. He was serious, a little closed off, and obviously valued honesty, but he also was sarcastic and funny. He wasn't a guy who you could never get to lighten up. He just seemed to flip back and forth between his feelings a lot. He was okay with being sarcastic and fun as long as it wasn't about anything important.

"Just so you're aware, I'm only eating outside because I could use some fresh air and not because you want to."

"Whoa." Quinn stopped walking, and Miles cocked his head at him.

"What?"

"I thought you didn't lie."

Miles rolled his eyes before he gently pushed around Quinn on his way to the sliding glass door. "Don't make me put a gag in you."

Oh. "Can we do that? I mean, not now because I don't want to be forced to shut up unless it's in bed, but maybe next time we fuck?"

Miles paused, with his hand on the door. His pupils were blown out as he looked like he was trying to figure Quinn out. "Are you being serious? Do you like to play like that?"

Quinn shrugged, swatted Miles's hand out of the way, and opened the door. "I'll leave you in suspense on that one."

Miles growled at him. "You drive me crazy."

"You drive me crazy too, Miles."

By the way Miles closed his eyes and quietly cursed, Quinn knew Miles realized Quinn had gotten him to say what they'd each refused to say in the bedroom, and he'd gotten Miles to say it first.

"You know what? I'm not sure I like you very much." Miles closed the door and set the food on the small, black iron table on the balcony.

"I know. You've told me. Only I don't believe you, Counselor. That's two lies."

Miles opened his mouth then closed it again as though he didn't know what to say next. God, this was fun. "I know. I'm a lot to handle. Sit down and eat. What are we doing after lunch?"

"Gagging you?" Miles answered as he took the seat across from him. Quinn began to pull the food out of the bags.

"No, not today. I'm not letting you off that easily."

"Um…working, then? I'm sure you have game stuff to do, and I have a case I need to work on."

Quinn's eyes shot up. "It's Saturday."

"So?"

"You can't work on weekends."

"You work on weekends," Miles countered.

"Yeah, but my job is fun."

"What the fuck?" Miles picked up a potsticker and threw it at him, bouncing it off his shoulder before it hit the balcony. Then he realized what he'd done because it definitely wasn't like him. He decided ignoring it was the best choice. "I like my job. I'm good as hell at my job."

"You're good at everything, except cooking. I know."

"If the shoe fits…" Miles replied, and Quinn rolled his eyes. When Miles took a deep breath, Quinn knew that brutal-honesty gig was about to be enacted. "This…spending time together. I can't promise you it will turn into anything."

"Did I ask for it to?" Quinn questioned. "And did I say I wanted it to?"

"Well, no. I'm just saying we don't have to rush things. We're not suddenly going steady."

Quinn frowned. "Does that mean I don't get your class ring?"

"Damn it!" Miles gritted out before a small smile touched at his lips. And then, he said something Quinn definitely didn't expect him to say. "I wish you were two," because it was again admitting that he saw something in Quinn that he liked, when at first, he'd hammered home to Quinn that this was nothing but sex.

"Eh. Maybe once you figure out my equation, I will be, and we'll both go our separate ways, and you can live a boring, surly existence again."

Miles didn't reply. After a moment, they both began eating. Every now and then, Miles would watch him. Quinn stuck his tongue out at him and Miles chuckled.

"Why are you looking at me like you don't know who I am?" Quinn finally asked.

"Because I don't know who you are."

That was a bullshit answer if Quinn ever heard one. "You know I like video games and I design them. That my best friend moved to Virginia to live with his Supercross boyfriend. You know I'm not a good cook and I'm a little obnoxious and I like to laugh. You know I was raised bouncing around from foster home to foster home and why. You know sometimes I can't sleep at night and that sometimes I come from a finger in my ass and nothing else. You know I like bruises on my hips and bossy tops and obviously Chinese food. Stop thinking so much. You know a lot about me."

"You know a lot about me too." There was this wonder in Miles's voice that told Quinn that knowledge shocked him. To realize the little things you came to know about someone just by talking to them, by fucking them. Sometimes those things added up to something and sometimes…well sometimes they apparently didn't come out to two.

The two of them finished eating. When they were finished, Quinn stood. The sun hurt his eyes slightly, though he didn't know why. There was a part of him that wanted to stay, but then he figured Miles was right. Maybe they were jumping in with both feet even though they didn't know what in the fuck they were jumping into.

"I guess I'll head out. I need to get a few things done. Later tonight, I'm going to Hotel Café. They have this local indie singer who plays there that I like, and I wouldn't want to keep you from your work." Quinn winked at him.

They went inside, and Miles stayed in the living room while Quinn went to his room and put his clothes back on.

A few minutes later he was standing by the door, with Miles's finger under his chin, tilting his head up.

Without a word, he pressed a quick kiss to Quinn's lips before stepping back and closing the door.

Well, he guessed that was that.

CHAPTER TWELVE

M ILES WAS BEING ridiculous.
He'd spent a couple hours trying to concentrate on work at home but hadn't had any luck. He'd paced and then cleaned the bathroom and imagined bending Quinn over the counter again and how his hot, tight ass felt wrapped around his dick and knew he had to get the fuck out of there before he lost his mind.

The thing was, it didn't get better when he got to the office. He thought about the talks they had and the sex they had and how they were just letting things happen to see where they went, and he was pretty fucking sure he was obsessed.

Miles obsessed about a lot of things—work, honesty, his friends.

He didn't obsess about a piece of ass but then, Quinn wasn't just a piece of ass, was he?

He'd become a friend. Miles cared about him, and that was some crazy fucking knowledge that he'd known but still didn't know what to do with.

For the hundredth time, he thought he was going to kill Quinn. Stupid, funny, sexy, sarcastic Quinn.

Yes, obviously he was obsessed.

"Argh!" Miles ran a hand over his buzzed head and picked up his cell phone.

Chance answered after the second ring. "What's up, boo?"

"I hate it when you call me that. It's so annoying. I'm not your boo."

There was a click, and Miles knew right away Chance had hung up on him. The fucker. He called right back, and the second Chance answered he said, "You hung up on me," as though it was new knowledge.

"That's because you were being a dick, and I wanted a do-over. Are you going to be nice now?"

Why was Miles friends with Chance again? "I can't make you any promises."

Chance sighed. "Well, that's a little better. Now, what's up, boo?"

Miles bit his lip, knowing that his friend said that just to annoy him, a small part of him appreciating it. None of their group let one another get away with anything, which if you asked Miles, was the way it should be. They called each other out on their shit, but usually it was Miles doing the calling out. He didn't like being on the other end of it.

What would they think if they knew about Quinn? How much shit would they give him? Especially Oliver, considering Miles has harassed him for years about being obsessed with Matt, and now Miles himself was obsessed. He shook that thought from his head. There was no reason to think about Chance, Oliver, and Matt knowing anything about Quinn. His sex life and his friendships had nothing to do with each other. "Not much," he finally answered. "Just working on a case and I needed a mental break so I thought I'd see what you're up to."

"Not a whole lot. I'm just hanging out a bit. I'm dancing at Vibe tonight. Wanna come watch?"

"No, I can't. Not tonight." Miles's answer came automatically even though it was a lie. He definitely could go watch Chance dance tonight. He likely should go watch him. It would help him get his mind off of someone else.

"You're ridiculous. Let me guess, you're going to bury yourself in law books and notes and cases because it's not Friday and that's the only night you have designated for fun, am I right?"

I've been having more fun than that. I've spent more than one night with a man and we had lunch together and I told him about my past... "Yes and there's nothing wrong with that." There went another lie. For someone who'd always prided himself on brutal honesty, he was becoming quite the liar.

"No, I guess there's not. One of us has to be the boring one."

"Hey! I'm not boring!"

"Well, I sure as shit am not the boring one. Ollie and Matt are shacked up, growing up and moving on, so they aren't boring. That leaves you."

Miles grinned and the first thought that slammed into his brain was, *Chance and Quinn would get along. Chance would love hanging out with Quinn.* "Fine. I'll be boring."

There was a pause and then Chance asked, "Are you sure

there's nothing going on with you lately? You haven't been yourself."

No, he really hadn't, and even though that should bother him, it strangely didn't as much as he thought it would. He could tell Chance what was going on. That he'd met a man who intrigued him. Chance would be happy for him. He would appropriately give Miles shit because that's what friends were for, but he would be happy for him. He would support him. If the situation were reversed, Miles would demand the information from Chance or Ollie or even Matt.

But then, why did he need to put a name to it and talk about it when it was basically nothing more than fucking the same person and hanging out with him? It wasn't as though he needed to make an announcement declaring his friends-with-benefits relationship with Quinn.

So, he didn't. He just said, "Yeah, I'm fine, baby. Why wouldn't I be?"

"I don't know. I'm just suddenly feeling out of the loop and I don't know why—first with Ollie and Matt and now with you. I don't like it. I'm supposed to be the center of attention, you know."

That made Miles laugh because it was true. He'd always been the one out of the four of them who demanded the most attention, just by being himself. "Aww. Is Chance feeling left out? Don't worry, we still love you."

"Well, duh," he answered, and Miles chuckled again. They got off the phone a moment later. Miles sat in his office chair, staring at his computer and then said, "Fuck it." He picked up his phone again and sent Quinn a text. **What time should I meet you at Hotel Café?**

Quinn's one word reply came almost immediately. **Nine.**

<div style="text-align:center">~~~</div>

QUINN HIT EVERY red light on La Cienega.

The text Miles had sent earlier partially came as a surprise and partially didn't. He'd been hopeful, though. Unlike Miles, it wasn't hard for Quinn to admit he liked him. That he enjoyed their banter just as much as he enjoyed their sex.

But then, Quinn was a totally different man than Miles was, and he strangely also liked that Miles did have such a hard shell to crack.

And somehow, Quinn was cracking the fuck out of it.

He wanted to continue doing it.

He pulled into the alley behind Hotel Café. The parking garage was across from it, security standing at the entrance and taking the parking fee. Once he paid, he parked and found his way to the doorway of the bar that opened in the alley rather than on the main street.

Music came from inside—the opening band, no doubt, as Quinn leaned against the building waiting for Miles to arrive.

He saw the black Lexus pull in, thought about walking over and meeting him but didn't. It was a few minutes later that Miles stepped out of the garage, and holy fuck, Quinn almost swallowed his goddamned tongue.

He wore a pair of black jeans and a black shirt with no collar and three silver buttons down the front. They were undone, giving a glimpse of his chest and all the smooth, brown skin. The sleeves were short, hugging his muscular arms.

He was taller than Quinn. It looked like he'd cleaned up his buzzed hair a little, not that he'd needed it, but his sides looked as though they faded more than before.

Miles commanded attention—men and women watched him as he looked around, and then his eyes met Quinn and a slow, sexy smile tugged at his lips.

Christ, he was fuckin' gorgeous.

He walked over with long strides, and Quinn told him, "I think everyone wants to drop to their knees for you, you fucking bastard."

"Do you?" Miles cocked a brow.

"Pretty boys always get me into trouble, so yes."

His brows pulled together and his forehead wrinkled as though he wasn't sure what he thought of Quinn's reply. "Are you going to tell me I look good?" Quinn asked. He'd rather ask questions than let Miles overthink things at the moment.

"You didn't tell me I looked good."

"I just called you pretty and said I wanted to get on my knees for you. What more do you want?" He still leaned against the building and crossed his arms.

"A demonstration?" Miles said then reached out and grabbed Quinn's hip. "You look good. You're always fucking gorgeous. That's what got us into this mess in the first place. Soon as I saw you, I wanted you beneath me."

Damned if Quinn's pulse didn't go erratic.

As soon as he'd seen Miles, he wanted to be beneath him as well.

Or to ride him—Quinn wasn't picky.

Miles's thumb brushed up under Quinn's dark blue tee and then under the edge of his jeans, where Miles's fingerprints were in his skin. "You're trouble," he added.

"Don't pretend you don't like being bad." Quinn heard the breathlessness in his own words. He liked being bad with Miles too.

"Oh, I'm not pretending anything. I'd duck down the alley with you right now, baby boy. Push you to your knees and take your mouth. Once I came in your mouth, I'd pull you to your feet and kiss you before I kneeled and made you come as well."

A strangled moan slipped past Quinn's lips. Why was that so goddamned hot? Having Miles call him baby boy and hearing what he wished he could do to Quinn.

And he would let him.

He played it off as though he wouldn't. "Tempting, but I'm in the mood to make you suffer." Quinn winked and Miles growled as Quinn stepped around him, making Miles's hand fall. "Let's go inside."

They waited in the short line and then entered the dark bar. There were low, gold glowing lights scattered across the room and against the walls. Small, round tables were in front of the black stage. Taller tables were littered about the room behind them.

Quinn led Miles to the bar. He was surprised when Miles

put his hand on the back of Quinn's neck as they waited, as though he just wanted to touch him. Or as though he wanted everyone to know Quinn was with him.

"What do you want?" Miles asked a few moments later when the bartender approached them.

"Oh, you're ordering my drink for me? Such a gentleman."

"I hate you," Miles said while squeezing Quinn's neck gently and then brushed his finger over the back of it. "Fine. I want a Jack and Coke."

"Two Jack and Cokes," Quinn told the bartender. While he made their drinks, Quinn turned around and leaned against the bar.

"So is this who we're here to see?" Miles asked and nodded backward toward the stage.

It was a band of three women who sounded a little bluesy. "No, but they're good too. We're here for Travesty. He's this young kid with an old soul. Kind of a mix of Bob Dylan, Leonard Cohen, and Jeff Buckley."

"Hmm." Miles shrugged, and Quinn wasn't sure if it was because he was interested or not. He reached over Quinn's shoulder and he realized the drinks were done. Miles grabbed them and Quinn turned around to pay, before Miles led them to a table in the back.

"So...do you come here often?" Miles asked when they sat, and Quinn rolled his eyes.

"That sounded very datey of you. We're on a date, aren't we?" Quinn teased back.

"I hate you," Miles answered, confirming they were, in

fact, on a date, even though Miles wasn't very happy with the idea.

"You don't date people you hate. That means you don't hate me. Stop pretending you do."

"Be quiet before I spank you."

"Is that supposed to make me stop? I'm afraid the threat will have the opposite result," Quinn teased and saw black fire brew in Miles's eyes. Before they could get off on that topic, he asked, "So, you're bi?" because he wanted to get to know more about Miles and he figured it was easier to do in public.

If Miles was surprised by the question, he didn't show it. "I am, but it's not often I'm with women. It's been a few years, in fact. I'm attracted to them, and have had sexual interest in them, but I typically lean more toward men."

"And your friends? You've known them most of your life?"

That question seemed a little more uncomfortable for Miles. He adjusted his position in his chair. "Yes. Our parents were friends. We grew up in a very affluent area. My mother and Chance's went to college together. My mother and Oliver's did a lot of charity work together. They were pregnant together—Ollie and Chance's moms, that is." He paused and took a drink. Quinn waited, knowing this wasn't easy on Miles. "My mother couldn't get pregnant. Chance had already been born—he's actually the oldest by a couple months. My parents got the call about me a little over a week before Ollie was born. We really had no other option except to be best friends. Even if we had, it wouldn't have changed anything. My mom used to tease us—she's into New Age stuff. She thought it was destiny—Oliver and Chance's moms being pregnant with boys and then her getting me. Add in that we're all gay or bi, and she was fucking convinced about some kind of higher power playing a role in our lives." Miles chuckled nostalgically. It was a good look on him—talking about his friends.

"What about the other one? Aren't there four of you?"

He nodded. "Matt came along later. His mother worked for Ollie's. Oliver fell in love with Matt at like twelve, and he's been there ever since."

"That's sweet," Quinn told him, meaning it. He didn't have that kind of meaningful friendship until he was older. That ended and from there it wasn't until college.

"It was a mess for a long time. Matt wasn't ready and frankly didn't deserve Oliver for years. I was always warning Ollie off him, trying to make him see what the rest of us did. Not that Matt was a bad man or as though it was all Matt's fault. He had some personal shit to deal with inside. Those aren't battles anyone else can face for you. Until Matt was willing to face them, they never would have been able to be together. Ollie never listened to me, though."

Miles telling Oliver how it was didn't come as a surprise to Quinn. "So you've always been bossy?" he asked before quickly adding, "And you've always taken care of people you love. I can see that." He wasn't sure if Miles realized he did that, but Quinn heard it in how he spoke about them, even during their first weekend together.

Miles paused, cocked his head slightly as though he hadn't

expected that and then nodded. "It's different now. Matty has his shit together. He's a good man. Not perfect but who in the fuck is? We're all flawed. Anyone who pretends otherwise is lying."

That was one of the things Quinn liked the most about Miles. He owned his shit. Not many people did that. It was a whole lot easier to judge.

Miles was...different. Special. He didn't think the other man knew it, though. Quinn realized it from the beginning. Not the full extent of course. Originally it had been mostly the fact that he was hot as hell and a good fuck, but he'd seen hints of more to Miles. Quinn had sensed that big fucking heart caged in his chest that he tried so hard to hide.

"You're a good man, Counselor."

Miles shrugged it off. "I have my moments like everyone else."

But Quinn could have sworn he was embarrassed.

CHAPTER THIRTEEN

MILES WAS TYPICALLY better at asking questions than he was answering them but he'd done his best for Quinn tonight. Quinn seemed to be satisfied, which oddly made Miles happy. "Are you this nosy on all your dates?" he asked while Quinn took a drink, and he damn near choked on it.

He set his glass down, patted on his chest, and coughed. "Nope. Just you. You're special." When Miles didn't reply, he continued. "What about me? Am I that special?" Which was obviously his way of giving Miles permission to ask questions of his own—not that he needed the okay, but he appreciated it.

"Did you always know you wanted to design video games?" He tried to tune out the music in the background and just listen to Quinn. Somehow, Quinn made the task easier than he thought it would be.

"I did. Games were a constant companion when people weren't always."

Because people hadn't been a constant in his life growing up—not the same people, at least. It made Miles realize how fucking lucky he was to have the friends and family he did. If anyone deserved that, it was Quinn.

"I was always smart, which was a plus. Kept my grades up even when I switched schools. I knew I wanted a different life than I had, and I saw an education as my way out of that. But I also knew it would never be a stuffy suit job for me—no offense."

God, he liked the man. He didn't cut Miles any slack. A lot of people were intimidated by him. "None taken," Miles replied.

"I applied for every grant, loan, and scholarship I could. Worked my ass off, and here I am. Fairly successful, sexy video game designer on a date with a gorgeous attorney."

"You sucking up to me?" Miles asked.

"Maybe." Quinn winked.

Life was such a roll of the dice sometimes. They both hadn't had the best start. Neither man had been raised by their blood family, yet their upbringings were so different. Miles could easily be Quinn, and Quinn could easily be Miles. Someone like his parents could have taken Quinn in, or Miles could have been unlucky enough that the call wasn't made to his family. You just never knew what life held.

"You did good. You should be proud of yourself." Miles respected the hell out of him. Quinn had his shit together. He didn't let his past affect his life.

"I am," Quinn replied.

He wanted to ask Quinn about his problem with sleep. What exactly had happened all those years ago? He knew he couldn't, though. It wasn't only because now wasn't the time, but even thinking about it made a protective instinct rip through him, tear him to shreds. He knew he'd want to protect Quinn from whatever had happened. Would want to take it away, but it wasn't as though he could fix something that happened in the past. Quinn was strong enough not to need him to, either.

It was then he realized the next act was taking the stage. He opened his mouth to ask another question, but Quinn cut him off, "Shh. This is my guy."

"I thought I was your guy?" It wasn't until the last word slipped past his lips that Miles considered what he said and what it meant, so he winked to play it off and ignored the wild run of his pulse. He wanted to be Quinn's guy. Wanted Quinn to be his. He'd never actually dated someone before. It had never been something he wanted.

"Tonight you're going to have to share me, Counselor."

"Hmm. I don't think so. I don't share well. I'm a stingy bastard when I want something." He waited for Quinn's reply because he'd just put out there that he wanted Quinn.

Like he knew Quinn wouldn't, he didn't let Miles's statement slip by. "And you want me."

"You knew that."

"You're making it sound a little different from what you said earlier."

Miles just shrugged and didn't deny what Quinn said— balls to the wall. He wasn't going to let himself turn into a liar.

"You always get what you want, don't you?" Quinn then took a sip of his drink, looking at Miles over the glass.

He thought about his life. In a lot of ways, he had everything he could ever want, but again, the truth ran off his tongue, because there was more he wished for. He wanted to know where he'd come from. "No, I don't."

The light in Quinn's eyes dimmed and Miles knew Quinn realized what he meant. "Well, I do," Quinn finally said. "I guess it's good that we want the same thing. Now be quiet before I'm the one gagging you."

Quinn watched the performance after that, and Miles found himself watching Quinn. Watching his lips move when he sang and his Adam's apple bob when he swallowed and feeling like something was wound around the two of them, binding them together.

And then he was a little embarrassed because he'd never thought something like that in his life, and thank God Quinn couldn't hear him.

Before he knew it, the performance was over and he had Quinn pinned against his car, hands squeezing his hips and his tongue sweeping Quinn's mouth.

He wanted to ravage him, to devour him. To fuck him over and over and over until they were nothing but two sweaty bodies melting into each other.

"My place or yours?" he asked before digging his teeth into Quinn's neck and savoring the shudder he was given in return.

"Slow your roll, Counselor," Quinn replied and Miles tensed up. "What makes you think I put out on the first date?"

"The fact that we fucked the first night we met?"

"That was different. That was sex. We're dating now."

"I changed my mind. I don't want to date you anymore."

Miles nuzzled into Quinn's neck again with a motherfucking smile on his face. The man could try to turn him down for sex and still somehow make him feel good.

"Too late. You're stuck now. I have to make you wait for it, make you so fucking crazy for a piece of my ass."

"Already there." Miles slid his hand behind Quinn and squeezed his cheek for emphasis. "I'm dying to get in it. I'd bend you over this car right now if you'd let me." He licked Quinn's collarbone.

Quinn rubbed his rock-hard erection against Miles. A low growl ripped from Quinn's throat. "I'm sure you would."

"You gonna give me your ass tonight, baby boy? I promise I'll be real good to it." Miles nipped the skin of his throat again and felt a tremble rock through Quinn. "I haven't gotten to taste it yet. I'll make a fucking feast of you." And he would. He couldn't fucking wait, actually.

Quinn tightened his hold on Miles before saying words Miles hadn't really expected to hear. "Not tonight."

It was then Miles realized he was serious. He pulled back and looked in Quinn's soft, kind eyes. "Really?" It was okay. It wasn't as though he wanted to fuck someone who wasn't feeling it, but he knew Quinn wanted him.

"It's been a big day. This isn't just fucking anymore. Just…make sure it's what you want because I know it's what I want. You got me all twisted up, Counselor." Quinn opened the car door, forcing Miles to step back.

It was what he wanted. God fucking help him, he wanted Quinn. Wanted to be with him, but Quinn was right. Today had been a big day, so he watched Quinn start his car.

He stepped back farther when Quinn pulled out of the parking spot. Watched while Quinn rolled down his window and grinned. "I already regret saying no, you sexy bastard." And then he drove off and yeah…Miles was smiling again.

"SO…YOU KNOW THAT really hot boyfriend of yours?" Quinn asked his friend Christian through the phone.

"No. Who would that be?" he replied, and Quinn rolled his eyes.

"None of that. I'm the funny one between the two of us, and you know it."

The other man laughed. Christian had a good sense of humor too, but Quinn would never admit it. "Whatever you say, but yes, I think I know who you mean."

"I kind of have one of my own. Well, not the same because hearts don't float by my head when I think about him. We're not devoting ourselves to each other on national television, which I'm still fucking jealous about, by the way, but we're dating." Beck had claimed Christian on TV after winning the AMA Championship. It had been pretty incredible to see.

Quinn added, "Oh, and he's hotter than Beck." There. Take that. Quinn might not get Supercross but Miles was fucking gorgeous. Not that Beck wasn't.

"First of all, no one is hotter than Beckett Monroe, and second, can we back this train up into the station? I'm fucking lost here. I think you need to start at the beginning."

Which he wouldn't have to do if Chris spent more time in LA, but he didn't say that. He was happy for Christian. He and Beckett deserved whatever joy they could find after being apart for so long.

"I'm seeing someone. He's...well, the fucking opposite of me in nearly every way. I'm not sure he's all that happy to be dating me but—"

"Fuck him then," Christian cut him off.

"No. Not like that." How did he explain it to Christian without telling Miles's story? It wasn't Quinn's to share. "He wants me. Don't kid yourself. I haven't changed that much since you left. I wouldn't be chasing someone who doesn't want me. He's just stubborn and surly and bossy as hell. Oh, and pretty."

"You're fucked."

"Right?" Quinn said. Christian knew his taste well. "I asked him to stay," Quinn admitted, and he knew Christian would know exactly what he was talking about.

"And you slept well?"

"All fucking night." It used to be Christian who did that for him when he struggled. He could squeeze out an hour or two around people he didn't trust, but it was restless. His body was tense, always ready to defend himself if he had to.

"Are you in love with him?" Christian asked, worry in his voice.

"I like him. I'm not looking to fall in love with him, and he sure as shit isn't looking to fall in love with me. He's got walls higher than a maximum-security prison, but I like him. And I got him to want to date me, which was a fucking struggle, let me tell you." They laughed and then the line went quiet. He wasn't sure why he'd called Christian to talk to him about Miles. Maybe because like Miles, Quinn only had a small number of people in his life who he truly trusted. Quinn was better at playing it off than Miles, probably because Miles didn't fucking try, but when it came to something important to him, there was only one person he wanted to talk to…and the truth was, Miles was important to him. That truth was hammered home even more when he'd wanted to go home with Miles last night but forced himself not to, because he wanted to give Miles that time to change his mind. The time to make sure he was cool with this because Quinn was obviously fucking thrilled about it. This phone call proved it.

"That's great, Quinn. I can't wait to meet him."

"Don't go that fast. I don't even know when you'll be out again and hell, this might be over in a week. Who knows?" But he hoped it wasn't.

"I'm not sure I like this guy."

"Aw, are you ready to defend my honor?" Quinn teased.

"Yes, yes I am."

Quinn chuckled and rolled his eyes. "Thanks, tough guy, but I'm all good. We're taking it slow. I just wanted to brag because you totally bragged when you got with dirt bike boy."

"No, I didn't!" Christian replied. He followed with, "Hey…be careful, okay? Make sure he's treating you the way you deserve."

Oh God. Quinn rolled his eyes. "Wow. That sounded very

older brother of you. I'm a big boy. I'm not going to let someone fuck around with me."

"Good. I really don't want to have to kick someone's ass. I'm too pretty to fight."

They went back and forth with that for a while before talking games. How fucking lucky was he to get to talk about games and it was work?

It wasn't long before they said their goodbyes and Quinn pulled his cell away from his ear to see a text from Miles.

I jerked off twice last night because of you.

He replied back, **Next time go for three.**

Fuck you.

You want to. Quinn wanted it too.

Obviously.

Soon, Counselor. I promise you, soon. He set his phone down. His chest felt lighter than it had before. He'd needed to hear from Miles. He'd needed to hear from him and hadn't realized it until he'd gotten the message from him.

Maybe he was more afraid than he wanted to admit that this would be over before it really began.

CHAPTER FOURTEEN

IT HAD BEEN the week from hell.

Miles spent nearly every day in court. He usually thrived on being in the courtroom. He loved the order of it, loved the fact that he was fucking good at what he did. In a lot of ways, this week had been no different and it still felt good as hell to fight and win. He was really tired too. He hadn't been able to see Quinn all week and he really fucking owed Miles for ditching him the other night.

Or that was the excuse he was giving himself, at least.

Maybe he just wanted to see Quinn. To laugh with him. And yes, also to fuck him. Quinn was a whole hell of a lot more fun than being in court, which wasn't something he admitted lightly, even if only to himself.

Now it was Friday night, and even though Miles didn't want to leave his apartment, he knew he would. Friday night happened no matter what.

He had just gotten out of the shower and wrapped a towel around his waist when his cell rang. It was plugged in beside his bed, so Miles walked over. He picked it up and grinned when he saw Quinn's name on the screen. Fucking grinned over a name on a screen. He was ridiculous.

"How's it going, Counselor?" Quinn asked when he answered.

"Exhausted." He fell back against his pillows. Jesus, it had been a long week. Why did he have to go out again?

"I can come over, bring you something to eat. You mentioned something about feasting on me the other night. I think we can make that happen. It'll be like the first weekend where we just fuck and chill all weekend. I'm beat too."

"Are you sleeping okay?" Miles asked, a tight fist around his chest. He'd feel like shit if Quinn had been struggling.

"Yeah," Quinn told him. "I'm fine, Daddy."

"Mmm. I like you calling me that."

"You would."

"You don't?"

"Could be fun," Quinn replied.

Yeah, it could be. Everything was fun with Quinn. Only it wouldn't happen. Not tonight, at least. "It's Friday. I'll be at Wild Side." Then as though he had to make an excuse for himself, he added, "I don't cancel on them. Ever." He couldn't. Not when it came to Oliver, Chance, and Matt. Maybe it didn't make sense to most people, but to Miles it did. They'd made a commitment to each other years ago. Friday night was their thing, and Miles didn't walk away from commitments. He didn't abandon people he cared about.

"Um…I'm pretty sure I didn't ask you to." There was a sharp edge to Quinn's voice that he hadn't had a moment before. It made Miles's defenses shoot up. What the fuck was his problem? Was he angry that Miles was keeping his commitment to his friends? That shit wouldn't fly with him.

"We don't bring other people either." Which was a shitty thing for him to say. Had he ever brought someone he was sleeping with to Wild Side? No. None of them had, but he also knew his friends wouldn't care. They'd probably fucking love it if Miles brought Quinn tonight.

"I'm pretty sure I didn't ask you if I could go either. Fuck you, Miles. I'm not some needy, weak man who needs you to invite me out or cancel on your friends for me. I just wasn't thinking about what day it was and I thought we could get together. If you don't want to, just say so. Don't start slinging excuses and accusations at me."

Quinn's words felt very much like an accusation, as well. "I'm not making excuses for anything. I just didn't know we had to hang out every weekend. Is that an obligation now? We decide to see where this goes, and now I have to defend going out with my friends?"

"What the fuck universe are you in right now? When did I ask you to defend going out with your friends? I asked if we could see each other. All you had to say was, *I have plans* and I would have teased you about...I don't know, something fucking stupid, but instead you're turning this into a big-ass deal when it doesn't need to be one. But as long as we're doing that, it's my turn. I'm not asking to meet your family. I'm not asking for a commitment. If this doesn't work, it doesn't work, but I will say, I sure as shit won't be a secret. You want to keep this going, I'm not going to be the guy you fuck every night but Friday because your goddamned friends can't know about me."

Miles's whole body went rigid. His muscles hurt they were so fucking tight. This was why he didn't do this shit. Why he didn't get close to anyone except Oliver, Chance, and Matt. "Don't bring them into it."

Quinn sighed. "Again, fuck you, Miles. I didn't bring them into anything. You're using them as a shield. Grow up. You want something, go for it. You don't? Sure as shit don't hide behind your friends. You made this a much bigger deal than it had to be."

Quinn hung up and it took everything inside of Miles not to throw his cell across the room. Instead, he squeezed it until his hand hurt. "Fuck!" he yelled in frustration. What in the hell just happened? He never should have played around with Quinn. At least he knew what to expect from his friends and they knew what to expect from him.

At least they never let him down.

"OH SHIT. WHO pissed you off?" Chance asked the second Miles fell into his seat at Wild Side. Lights flashed around them. Music blasted. People kissed and danced and Miles wanted nothing except to walk out.

"No one. I'm fine." He looked over and saw Austin, Dare's boyfriend, sitting at the table and wanted to ask what in the fuck he was doing here. Miles had no problem with the guy, but now he was joining them at their table or what?

"Austin and I are working on a fundraiser for the LGBT

center," Oliver told him as though he could read Miles's mind. Fundraising was something he'd become passionate about lately. He started when Matt went back to New York and Ollie was trying to get over him. It was something Oliver did for himself and Miles was damn proud of that, but right now, it just annoyed him because it put Austin at their table and made a quiet voice whisper in the back of his head...*if Austin was sitting with them, so could Quinn...*

Fuck that voice.

"I'll give you more information soon, but be prepared because I want you to be a sponsor. You—"

"It's fine. I'll do it. Whatever you need." Miles waved a hand at him. It was the last thing he wanted to discuss right now, and Oliver knew Miles would always help. "Why didn't you guys get me a drink? I'm fucking thirsty. Everyone else has a goddamned drink."

All eyes at the table were on him. He was being a dick and he knew it, but Quinn had been too. What in the fuck was his problem? Miles spent Friday night with his friends. The fucking end.

"Oh no. You're fine. 'No one pissed you off,' says Miles as he spits fire at everyone at the table," Chance said. "Anyone have some water to put out these flames?"

"Chance," Ollie warned and Miles rolled his eyes. They all fit into their roles but tonight, he was having none of it.

Miles looked at Oliver. "I don't need you to take care of Chance for me. I know how to deal with my own friend."

"What the fuck is your problem?" Oliver asked. "You're

being a prick." He absolutely was, only he couldn't seem to stop himself.

"Can we get back to the part where people are trying to *take care of* Chance? I don't need any of you to take care of me," Chance added. "I'll say what I want, when I want." As much as they all loved each other, they sometimes fought like brothers. In a lot of ways, they were brothers. All except for Ollie and Matt, of course.

"Okay, I think we all need to calm down." Matt wrapped a protective arm around Oliver.

Was he fucking kidding? "We fight sometimes, Matty. It's what we do. I get that you ran away for ten years but—"

"Stop. Right there," Oliver cut Miles off. "You keep going and you're going to piss me off and you won't like it, Miles. Don't take whatever is wrong with you out on Matt."

"Oh, of course you're going to take his side." Like Ollie had ever taken anyone's side over Matt's.

"I'm going to go get you a drink." Austin stood and walked away.

Miles's heart was beating too fast, like it would burst through the walls of his chest. Why the hell was he letting this bother him so much? He'd gotten in a fight with Quinn. Big fucking deal. He hardly knew the guy. Thank God their…continued fucking or whatever it was, ended before it really started. Miles didn't have time for this kind of shit.

"Take Matt's side? Can you stop sounding like you're twelve now? Jesus, you're being a dick, Miles, and you know how much I like dick," Chance told him. "But right now, I don't like you. What the hell is wrong with you?"

"Fuck," he gritted out and then dropped his head against the seat. His hands were shaking but he didn't know why. Why was he so angry? Why did he care so much that he and Quinn were done? It didn't make sense. He shouldn't be taking shit out on his friends when they were the most important people in his world.

"I think we need to have a family meeting," Chance said, but Miles didn't reply.

"What's wrong, Miles? You're obviously upset. Want to go to Chance's?" His apartment was the closest to Wild Side. Miles had dragged Ollie there himself to talk to him about Matt a few months before and, now Oliver attempted to do the same thing to Miles.

"No. I'm fine," he answered. He had no reason not to be fine. Why didn't he feel fine?

"If one of us would have walked in here like that, you would have forced our ass to tell you what was wrong. Why do rules apply to us and not you?" Oliver asked. Leave it to him to be logical.

"Because I'm an asshole and you aren't." And he'd been such a fucking prick to Quinn tonight, hadn't he? He'd treated Quinn badly and now he was doing the same thing to them.

"No," Oliver said. "You're a caretaker just like I am. You've always given me shit for that and you don't realize you're the same way. You want to protect people you love just like me, but the difference is, you don't admit it and you don't accept it in return. You'd do anything for the three of us but won't let us do anything for you."

"He's right," Matt said from beside him. He was right. They all were. Miles knew that.

He looked up when Austin set a drink down in front of him. He smiled at Miles, kindness in his eyes, and Miles tried to apologize with his. Austin didn't deserve to get caught up in Miles's shit.

Austin nodded, understanding in his kind eyes, and disappeared, leaving them to their table, the business of the bar somehow muted around them.

Miles exhaled a heavy breath. He was going to do this. He was really going to attempt to explain some of it. "I got in an argument with someone, and I'm upset. I'm sorry I took it out on you guys."

"Your parents?" Oliver asked, and he shook his head.

"Who?" Chance questioned. "You don't socialize with anyone else enough to argue with them."

"Chance!" Oliver warned again.

"What? It's true," he countered, and damned if Miles didn't think again about how much Chance and Quinn would get along.

"Just someone," Miles answered. "I don't want to talk about it because I haven't figured it out myself yet." The answer should be simple. It was because he liked Quinn. He knew that. He'd admitted that to Quinn and to himself. He just didn't think he realized how much until they'd argued. Until he was faced with the truth that this might already be over. "I won't take it out on you guys again, though."

That was the best he could give. They obviously knew it because the three men around him nodded.

They had a few drinks after that. There was talking and laughing and joking but the evening held a somber tone to it as well. Miles couldn't make himself enjoy their night the way he always did. The longer they stayed, the worse he felt. The more he thought, the less he liked the train of his thoughts.

It was a few hours later when they stood on Robertson Boulevard saying their goodbyes. Just as Miles was about to walk away, Matt gently grabbed his wrist. Chance and Oliver were involved in a conversation of their own, so they didn't hear when Matt lowered his voice and said, "I know we've never been the closest out of the four of us…but I'm here. If you ever want to talk, I'm here."

That had taken a lot for Matt to say. Miles knew it. "Thank you," he replied. "I appreciate that." And he really did.

Miles went home, sat on his balcony, and watched the city beneath him. He didn't sleep all night.

CHAPTER FIFTEEN

Q UINN'S EYES BURNED.
He'd spent the whole night on his computer, fucking around with a game. A plate with crusted food from his dinner last night sat on his desk. The coffee pot was empty, the last cup going cold by his keyboard.

When he leaned back in his chair, his neck ached. He attempted to rub out the stiffness while trying to ignore the fact that he'd sat in this fucking chair all night, not because he'd wanted to work so damn badly, but because he was upset about Miles.

About the argument, about the realization he'd gotten hurt. And why in the hell had he gotten so tangled up in the other man? It shouldn't have mattered. It shouldn't have affected any part of his body other than his dick, but it did, and he was pissed at Miles for fucking it up before they had the chance to really get started.

Well shit. Here he was obsessing about the very thing he told himself he wasn't going to think about.

Quinn pushed out of the chair and made his way into the en suite. He got the shower going—hot as he could take it because there was nothing like a hot shower early in the morning to wake your ass up.

He relaxed under the fiery spray of water and let it try to seep in through his pores. He cleaned up, then washed his hair before turning the water off.

Quinn took care of his morning routine as though it was later than seven in the morning or he had somewhere he needed to be, likely because he didn't know what else to do. He needed to keep himself busy somehow.

Fucking Miles. He was going to kick his ass. What did he have to be so goddamned scared about? Why couldn't he just let Quinn in? Tell him he had plans last night but hey, maybe we can do something tomorrow. That's all he'd had to say.

Quinn pulled a pair of white boxer briefs out of his drawer and pulled them on. He'd just finished slipping on a pair of worn blue jeans when a knock sounded from his living room. A tingle started at the base of his spine, and shot up his back, because somehow he knew, *fucking knew* who it was.

And he was pissed.

There was a part of him that was relieved too, even if it was only because he could tell Miles to grow up in person.

He stomped like an angry toddler into the other room, as though Miles could see his ridiculous tantrum. Without looking through the peephole, he jerked the door open. Miles's eyes immediately bore into him, held him, and they were filled with confusion and sadness and maybe a little anger, but Quinn didn't think about him. No, he was angry at him-self...and he was here. At seven on a Saturday morning, he was here.

"You didn't sleep," Miles said, and it sort of jerked him out of his anger, made him falter because there was nothing but concern in Miles's voice. They hadn't really known one another very long, yet he'd taken one look at Quinn and knew. More than that, it bothered him. It obviously upset Miles.

"No, I didn't. It's not because I was pissed off at this guy I know. He's a real fucking prick, but I was up because I was working." *Liar, liar, liar.*

"He knows he's a prick," Miles answered, and Quinn already felt his defenses softening. goddamn Miles.

"Then he needs to do something about it. At least if he plans to be in my life. I don't play games. Not when shit matters."

Miles sighed and rubbed a hand over his head and, for a moment, Quinn thought he was going to walk away.

"What do you have to be so fucking scared of, Miles? Make me understand."

"I don't know!" His voice was rough, louder than it had been a moment before. "I don't know," he said more softly this time and then pushed his way into Quinn's apartment. "Emotions don't always make sense. They're not logical."

In that, Miles was right. Quinn closed the door behind him and dropped his head back, looking at the ceiling. Jesus, what in the fuck were they getting into?

When he turned, he saw Miles standing by the window, looking out over Los Angeles. His hand was flat against the wall beside it as he stared out. "Besides my parents, there are three people in this world who I've ever let matter to me—I mean, really fucking matter. Matter enough to influence me."

Chance, Oliver, and Matt. Quinn knew that. There was a part of him that was jealous about it, too.

"It wasn't even as though I had a real choice with them—Ollie and Chance, at least. They were always there. They were always a part of my life. I don't know my world without them. Matt was harder for me because he *wasn't* always there. He came after but he was important to Ollie, so he became important to me."

Because that was the kind of man Miles was. He had a hard exterior but he was soft inside. He cared about people. He cared about his friends, probably more than most people realized. But if Quinn was going to do this with him, if they were going to give this a try, he wouldn't settle for being second string.

"And? What does that have to do with me? Do you want to keep me separate from your life? We can hide away in our apartments and fuck like crazy, but that's the extent of it? Do you think I'm going to try and get involved in your friendships with them? Come between you? Jesus, Miles. It wasn't ever about that. I understand if you want to cancel and I sure as shit am not a dog that is always going to be at your feet. I don't need to follow you and your boys around but I won't be a secret either. That's all I was trying to say. It needs to be a possibility. I spent my life bouncing around from home to home. I didn't have meaningful relationships. I didn't matter to those people. I won't spend my time with someone if I don't matter to them."

Miles didn't look up. In fact, he bowed his head more, keeping his back to Quinn. "You matter to me. That's why this is so fucking hard. Because you matter and most people don't." He turned on Quinn then, his eyes wild like he was standing on the edge. "I've never had to juggle someone else, and my friends. I've never had to bring someone else in. No one else was important enough."

"Fuck that," Quinn replied. He wasn't going to let Miles take the easy way out of this. He wasn't going to let him hide behind his friendship. He walked over to Miles then, saw his chest rise and fall through this T-shirt. "Don't pretend this is about them. This is about you. Grow the fuck up and say what you're really feeling."

"Don't—"

"No. You don't. You're in or you're out. This might have started out just being some random hookup, but we both know that's not where it is now. I don't know where the hell it could go. I'm not saying I'm in love with you. I'm not saying I expect a long-term commitment from you. I'm saying we really see where this could go—not just in words, like at Hotel Café, but actions, Miles, or we walk the fuck away." Because he wasn't going to let himself get any more involved unless they were on the same page. "What the hell are you so afraid of?"

"Being alone," Miles gritted out. "Being left behind." He tried to turn, but Quinn grabbed his wrist and held tightly. There was a flash of anger in Miles's whiskey eyes. He didn't think most people stepped up to Miles this way, but Quinn sure as shit would. He might like being dominated when he fucked, but not here.

"You think I'm not scared of the same shit? That's likely part of the reason we're both here right now, why we connected with each other, and why we're in this position in the first place. You're not the only person in the world who's been hurt, Miles. You're not the only person who's been left behind."

"Your mom died. That's different. It wasn't—"

"Thirteen," Quinn cut him off.

"Thirteen what?"

"I was in thirteen different homes. Thirteen people sent me away. Walked away from me. This isn't a competition. It's not a game of who's been hurt the most. We both have scars, but we're still standing. The question is, are you going to spend your whole life punishing yourself or are you going to move on?"

He hardly had time to take a breath before Miles jerked him closer and crashed their mouths together. He moaned, and Miles's tongue pushed past his lips. Rough hands grabbed his ass, squeezed and then ran up his back and tangled in his hair.

Miles used his hold to pull Quinn's head back, and he got the burn he loved so damn much.

"What the fuck do you do to me?" Miles asked, and then they were kissing again. Hungry, needy kisses that went straight to Quinn's cock.

"How do you make me want you so much?" Miles said into his neck before biting him there.

"Why are you so goddamned intriguing? Why do I feel like I know you in ways I don't know anyone else?" He pushed his hand down the back of Quinn's jeans, ran his finger down Quinn's ass crack.

Strong arms wrapped around him, lifted Quinn so he wrapped his legs around Miles's waist.

"I'm sorry. You got my head all fucked up, and I don't know how to deal with it."

They were moving then, as Miles carried Quinn toward his bedroom.

"You got me thinking things I've never thought about before. Part of me wants to spank your tight little ass for it and the other part worries I won't be able to breathe if I can't see where this might go."

"Oh fuck," Quinn said, a wild stampede in his chest. "How'd you get so good at sweet talk? You're gonna make me even more crazy about you than I already am."

Miles dropped him to the bed. "You'd rather dirty talk? Wanna know that I'm gonna treat you real good to make up for being a prick? Gonna play with your little hole just the way you like, bring you to the edge and pull you back again till your balls are so damn tight, and you're begging me to let you shoot your load."

"Fuck." Quinn's eyes rolled back, and he bucked his hips, needing exactly what Miles promised to give him.

"You good? You ready for me?" Miles asked as he played with the opening in Quinn's jeans. He'd never gotten around to buttoning and zipping them.

"Yeah," he answered, his eyes firmly on Miles. The other man looked back at him, stared hard like he was trying to apologize with them, like he was making a commitment to do better because he felt the same need Quinn did.

"See? Always such a good boy." Miles winked at him and then pulled Quinn's jeans and underwear off. His cock was red and leaking all over his stomach already. He lay sideways, with his legs over the side of the bed, Miles standing between them. "Don't worry. I'll play with you, too." Miles ran his finger up Quinn's dick—root to tip.

"You're killing me," Quinn told him.

"I know, baby boy."

Miles reached in Quinn's nightstand and grabbed the bottle of lube there. "Lift your hips up," he commanded before reaching for Quinn's pillows next. He propped them under Quinn so his ass was in the air, his upper body slanted downward where he lay on the bed. "Spread your legs for me real good."

There was zero chance Quinn would argue with that. He opened his legs as Miles squeezed lube into both his hands. Two fingers from his left hand went straight to Quinn's hole. He rubbed it gently, like he just wanted to tease Quinn as he used two fingers on his right hand to dance up and down Quinn's dick.

"Oh fuck," he said again. They seemed to be the only two words his brain could make as he shuddered and his eyes rolled back at Miles's tender touch. Somehow, these two small touches mesmerized him. They were everything, and he felt them caressing every part of his body.

"Look at me," he ordered, and Quinn tried like crazy to

keep his eyes open. Their stare stayed locked on each other as Miles teased his ass, oh-so-fucking-good while his other hand played with Quinn's cock. "Feel good?" Miles asked.

"You know it does. You just want to hear me say it."

"Then say it," Miles replied.

"Jesus, you feel so fucking good," Quinn admitted. He was so fucking good at this. At making Quinn go crazy with pleasure.

He damn near melted into the bed when Miles wrapped a hand around his erection and pushed two fingers into his hole at the same time.

He was on sensory overload with all of Miles's attention on him—his ass, his dick, and those brown eyes that entranced him so much.

Miles pushed his fingers deep, rubbed Quinn's prostate as he jacked him slowly. Quinn felt his orgasm building already, it was there, so fucking close—this explosion inside of him that would detonate in three, two, "Fuck!" he yelled when Miles pulled his fingers out and let go of his prick. "What the hell are you doing?" He'd been right there...right fucking there when Miles stopped.

"Playing," Miles answered simply and then he started to do it again. He pet Quinn's hole, rubbed his fingers around the rim as his fingers tickled up and down his dick. Then he was stroking him again, finger-fucking him until Quinn was right on the brink, ready to blow his load all over his stomach when Miles pulled back again.

After the third time, he couldn't breathe. His chest hurt

and he was dizzy. He felt like he'd been transported to another universe. Like there was no gravity and Miles was tethering him down. "Please…" he begged. "Oh, fuck, Miles. I need to come. I'm losing my mind." His eyes fluttered, and Miles swatted his thigh.

"Look at me."

Quinn managed to pry his eyes open again.

With his fingers still in Quinn's ass, Miles let go of Quinn's erection and palmed his own through his jeans. "You want this?"

"Yes, motherfucker. You know I do."

"Aww. That's not a very good boy," Miles teased. "I'm being so nice to you. Treating you so well, and you're going to talk to me like that?"

Quinn wasn't sure where Miles was going with this, how far he liked to take these games. "I'm sorry, sir," he chanced, and Miles's eyes damn near started to glow.

The air around them changed. It still popped and crackled with sexual energy but then it was suddenly laced with more emotion. Like the conversation had suddenly changed. Miles's gaze softened, morphed to something that Quinn didn't understand. The only thing he did know was that it was *more*. "I'm sorry, too." Miles said, his voice rough and emotional. "I'm sorry, too," he repeated, obviously speaking about last night.

Quinn smiled at him, and whispered, "I know." There wasn't a part of him that doubted it.

CHAPTER SIXTEEN

QUINN WAS MAKING him lose his mind.

Miles felt shit he wasn't used to feeling, and he wanted to make sure Quinn knew he was sorry. That he'd do his best not to fuck up again, because the other option was walking away from Quinn, and Miles knew he wasn't ready for that.

He felt tied to this man in ways he'd never been attached to anyone else. Last night, the binds had felt too tight…today, they weren't tight enough.

"Are you going to fuck me or what?" Quinn asked, pulling Miles out of his thoughts.

Yeah…he was. He wanted his dick so far in Quinn's ass, he'd feel him there for days. It amped him up that Quinn liked to play the way he did. That they were submissive and dominant by nature, even though he wouldn't go as far as to say either of them were in the lifestyle. They just liked what they liked, and those desires molded together well. Fit together the way you could only hope you'd fit with someone else.

"Turn over," Miles told him as he grabbed a condom from the drawer. He shucked his jeans and underwear off then pulled his shirt over his head as Quinn rolled onto his belly, legs spread and ass waiting for him.

Miles rolled the condom down his aching erection, then stroked it with a freshly lubed hand. He reached out and spread Quinn's cheeks, looked at his pucker, and damn near lost his balance. "Freshly shaved hole. You were waiting for me?"

"Was hoping," Quinn replied, breathlessly.

Miles rubbed his thumb against it. "So fucking sexy. I can't wait to stretch your pink little hole with my cock."

"Then do it."

His fucking pleasure. Miles grabbed the base of his erection, opened Quinn up with the head of his dick. He watched it stretch to accommodate him, watched as inch after inch of his dick disappeared between Quinn's pale cheeks. He suddenly wanted to see them red, so he smacked his right cheek, over and over in rapid succession as Quinn wiggled beneath him, thrusting against the bed.

"Yes. Miles. God, that feels so fucking good."

When that cheek was good and red, Miles moved to the left, paying it the same attention. His cock twitched each time the smacking sound echoed through the room. As Quinn's skin got pinker and pinker.

When Quinn's whole ass was crimson, he pushed his dick in deep again, damn near blowing his load the second he was tucked all the way inside. He was on the ragged edge, wanting his orgasm to take him over right now but needing more at the same time.

He pulled almost all the way out and watched as his dick

opened Quinn up again. Watched their bodies come together. Felt something low and deep in his gut that he didn't understand.

Even though he loved seeing Quinn's red ass while he fucked him, Miles pulled out, flipped him over and shoved Quinn's legs back before he pushed inside again.

He leaned forward, mouth close to Quinn's ear as he rutted against him. "I never got it before…wanting the same person more than once, but I don't know if I'll ever get enough of you."

It wasn't an admission that was easy to make, that he couldn't see a place in the future where he wouldn't want to be inside of Quinn. It would happen, right? He'd get his fill of Quinn, and Quinn would get his fill of Miles as well. It had to happen.

"Yeah…yeah, me too," Quinn replied, and then their mouths were pushed together and their tongues were battling. Their bodies were slapping against one another and, motherfucker, did Quinn's ass feel just right wrapped around Miles's dick.

Quinn ripped his mouth away. "Oh, fuck. I'm gonna come. Jerk me off, Miles."

He leaned up enough to shove a hand between them. He gripped Quinn's cock—hard and hot as a rock in the sun and began stroking it. His balls were on fire he wanted to come so badly, but it wasn't until he felt the hot spurt of Quinn's jizz on his hand, running through his fingers that Miles gave in. That he took a dive over the edge, his orgasm blazing through him and setting him on fire.

He fell against Quinn then, pulled his hand up, and licked Quinn's come off his fingers. When he finished, Quinn leaned forward and kissed him. Miles let him run the kiss, let him suck Miles's tongue and nibble at his lips.

When Quinn had his fill, he held the back of Miles's head as Miles lay on him. "Will you go to Wild Side with me on Friday?" he asked. He didn't let himself think. Didn't let himself worry. He just gave himself this moment and the man he wanted so fucking much.

"Only if you really want me there, not if it's out of some strange obligation. That's never what it was about," Quinn replied. "You can hang out with your friends every Friday without me as long as it's because that's your routine and not because you're not fully letting me into your life."

"I know." God help him, he wanted Quinn to go with him. Wanted to see him laugh with Chance.

"Then yes." He paused, before adding, "God, you fucked me good. I don't think I'll ever be able to move."

"Then you don't have to." Miles stood up, pulled his condom off, and tossed it in the trash. He lifted Quinn, put him in the middle of the bed, and then lay down beside him.

He ran his hand through Quinn's hair. Palmed his sweaty balls. Rubbed the drying come on his stomach. He was addicted to him. He wanted to devour him. Wanted to know everything there was to know about him.

"Does this mean you're my boyfriend now?" Quinn asked, and Miles froze. Boyfriend? Wow…

Quinn's loud laughter broke apart all Miles thoughts. "You fucker." He smacked Quinn's thigh again.

"You know you wanna be my boyfriend," he teased.

"You sound like you're sixteen."

The fucked-up part was, Miles thought he probably did. He'd always wondered what in the hell Ollie had been thinking when it came to Matt. Not that Miles was in love with Quinn, but he hadn't understood that commitment Oliver had wanted to make to Matt. How he'd wanted to trust in someone so damn much on a different playing field than the friendship between them.

That's what being here meant he wanted. That's what inviting Quinn to Wild Side meant he wanted.

"Isn't that the same as my admission that I wanted to date you?" he asked.

"Nope. It's different. Are you admitting it?" He turned his head to look at Miles, those kind eyes that Miles had first noticed ensnaring him.

"Yes, I'm admitting it. I'm pretty sure fucking you the way I did was my way of claiming you, but if you need me to say more, I will." Brutal fucking honesty. It was time to get back to who Miles was.

"I think the way I begged you to fuck me was my way of doing the same."

Miles let out a relieved breath, surprised that he'd held it. They were admitting the same thing. They wanted the same thing.

"This is fucking weird. I'm not the boyfriend type. You are

doing some strange shit to me," he said, and Quinn laughed.

"Just go with it. Whatever happens, happens. We still haven't fallen in love with each other, so we're safe."

And Miles was pretty much done with this conversation. He'd done enough sharing and caring for one day. "Go to sleep, baby boy. Your eyes look tired." He owed Quinn some rest after last night.

He wrapped his arm around Quinn, turned, as did Quinn, so his ass was tucked against Miles's groin, and they went to sleep.

THEY SLEPT FOR hours. Other than that, they spent most of Saturday and Sunday the same way they'd spent their first weekend together—fucking and eating, but this time, they played some more of the video game Quinn had played with Miles before.

They didn't talk about anything important. He figured they'd had enough of that earlier. Miles had no doubt hit his quota for the day...week, hell, maybe even the month.

It was around seven when they ordered a pizza. The two of them played a little more of the game, before Quinn asked, "So, you wanna have a sleepover at my house again tonight, or what?"

Miles rolled his eyes. "You need to have yourself checked." A smile teased his lips.

"Checked how? You did a prostate exam earlier and that seemed fine—ouch, stop it!" he said when Miles practically leaped onto him from his seat beside Quinn on the couch. He pushed Quinn until he lay down and straddled his hips and leaned forward.

"Your asshole's just fine. It's your brain I'm worried about."

"Why? Because I like you?" Quinn joked.

"No. Because you're psychotic." Miles nudged Quinn's nose with his own, brushed his lips across Quinn's cheek. "I'm impossible not to like…you on the other hand…"

Quinn wrapped his arms around Miles. "I think you have that backward."

"You think so, huh?" Miles asked, his voice sexy and raspy and, Jesus fucking Christ, he got Quinn hard. When his lips slowly teased Quinn's open, he was ready to go ass up again even though he was already tender, but then the doorbell rang and Miles growled.

"Get up. We need food."

Miles climbed off him. Quinn made it almost all the way to the door, before Miles replied, "I'll need to be up early so I can go home to get ready for work."

He turned and winked at Miles. "I think we can work with that, Counselor." They ate pizza and showered together. Quinn tried to pretend he wasn't paying attention as Miles spoke to Oliver when he called. Miles apologized again for Friday night, and Quinn wondered what had happened. If he'd told his friends about Quinn and their fight and holy fuck, he was doing a lot of worrying and thinking when it came to Miles Sorenson.

After dinner, they hung out for a while and blew each other before going to sleep. The second Miles's phone alarm sounded the next morning, Quinn felt the bed shift. Miles tried to get up, but he reached out and grabbed him.

"You're in an awfully big hurry, Counselor." Quinn ran his nose along Miles's stubbled jawline.

"Don't start something we won't have time to finish." But it was Miles who grabbed Quinn and pulled him on top of him. "I have to go to work."

"Call in," Quinn said on the fly.

He could see the absolute horror on Miles's face. "I can't call in."

Oh God. This was going to be fun. "I'm pretty sure you can." He touched Miles's forehead. "Oh, look at that, you feel hot."

"I am hot."

"Cocky bastard."

"I have to go to work," Miles countered.

"Do you have to be in court today?"

Miles paused. Two small wrinkles formed between his eyes as though he was thinking…considering. Bingo.

"No…but I've never called in sick before in my life."

Good God. "You're a stick in the mud. You're calling in and you're going…hmmm, to the beach with me. I'll let you rub suntan lotion on my back and watch your dick get hard in your Speedo." He wasn't sure why he hadn't thought of it sooner. This sounded like the perfect day to Quinn.

"I'm not boring, fuck you very much. I'm responsible and

we can go to the beach this weekend."

"We can also go to the beach today. It's what boyfriends do."

"Oh, for fuck's sake." Miles playfully rolled his eyes. "Boyfriends go to the beach together? Is that in the rule book? Don't make me break up with you—and stop saying that. It's weird."

"You're the one who likes rule books and not me. Also, what's weird? That you're my boyfriend?" Quinn countered. "That you spent a weekend with me and never stopped thinking about me and my delectable ass. That the second you saw me at Wild Side a few weeks ago you had to have me? Then you begged to date me and now you've begged to be my boyfriend? No, I won't say any of that." He winked... "Boyfriend."

Miles growled, and before Quinn realized what was happening, he flipped them. Quinn's legs fell open, and Miles's hips were tugged between them. "You keep talking like that and I won't go as easy on your ass as I did yesterday."

"Fucking or spanking?" Quinn asked. He was down for either.

"You're insatiable." Miles sounded almost awed. Quinn liked the sound from him. He liked everything about Miles...except when he was being an asshole, that was.

"I'm not sure that's something you should be complaining about. I mean, I can change it if you want. Oh! Maybe we should try that abstinence thing," Quinn joked.

Miles didn't reply, obviously knowing that Quinn wasn't

serious. He just buried his face in Quinn's neck and bit the meaty spot where it met his shoulder and then licked the pain away.

He was considering calling off. Quinn could feel it.

"What kind of spell have you cast on me? I hardly recognize myself."

Quinn didn't know, but whatever it was, Miles had cast the same spell on him.

CHAPTER SEVENTEEN

IT WASN'T LONG after Miles had made the call to work when his cell rang. Quinn's head was in his lap, his lips stretched around Miles's cock. He craved this man all the time—the heat of his talented mouth. The way he licked at Miles's crown before sucking him deep again. Fuck yes, calling in had been the best idea Quinn had ever had.

When his phone rang again and Quinn looked up at him from where he lay between Miles's legs, mouth full of dick, he smiled around it and damned if Miles's heart didn't jump. Fucking jumped. He was so screwed when it came to Quinn.

"You gonna get that?" Quinn asked as he moved down to tongue Miles's sac.

"It's my mom, so I'd rather not." He didn't have to look at the screen to know it was her, and talking to his mother while—*oh fuck* that felt good—Quinn sucked his balls wasn't something he really wanted to do.

He tangled his hand in Quinn's hair, guiding him. The call ended but immediately began ringing again. Quinn sighed, leaned on his elbow, and said, "You get it. I'll pick up where I left off when you're done."

Christ, he was getting cock-blocked by his mom. "Hello?"

he said, ridiculously trying to make his voice sound rougher than it usually did. Should he fake a cough? Moan? No, that might be overkill.

"Dad said you're sick and you called off work. You've never called in. What's wrong, baby?" she asked just as Quinn's tongue ran from the base of his cock to the head.

Miles narrowed his eyes at him, and Quinn shrugged and whispered, "I'm an impatient motherfucker and I really like your cock."

He sucked the head and Miles nearly shot off the bed. He was going to kick Quinn's ass for blowing him while he was on the phone with his mom.

"I'm fine...*fuck*—I mean. Yeah...I'm sick." And then he did it, faked a goddamned cough.

When Quinn chuckled softly, Miles narrowed his eyes at him.

"You've been sick before and you've never called in. Do you want me to come over? I can bring you some chicken soup or take you to the doctor."

"I'm fine, Mom," he said and fisted his hand in Quinn's hair again, pushing him lower on his dick. He couldn't have a mouth on his cock and not take advantage. It didn't matter who was on the phone.

"You sound out of breath. I'm worried about you."

Quinn swallowed around the head of his dick, deep throating him like a fucking champ. "Oh God...I'm fine...don't come...over...I gotta go. I'll call you later." Miles ended the call, thrust his hips, held Quinn's head, and spilled down his throat.

The second Quinn came up for air, Miles told him, "I'm going to kill you…just as soon as I can move again."

"You wouldn't kill me. You like me too much." Quinn winked, jumped out of bed, and Miles watched his sexy ass as he walked into the bathroom.

Yeah, he did like him too much. Damn it.

THEY SHOWERED, HAD breakfast, and then went to Miles's house for him to pack a bag for the beach. He still couldn't believe he was doing this. It was just a trip to the beach, so it shouldn't be a big deal but it was a trip to the water on a fucking Monday when he should be at work.

They made it to Miles's car and to the 101 freeway before his cell rang again. "Oh fuck." Miles rolled his eyes after looking at the screen.

"Your mom again?" Quinn asked from the passenger seat, snickering. "She offered to bring you chicken soup while I was blowing you. That's some funny shit."

"No," Miles replied. "Worse. It's Chance." Who he had no doubt called because he'd gotten notice that Miles called off work today. Maybe this whole close-friendship-like-family thing wasn't such a good idea after all. "What?" Miles said into the cell.

"You better be dying."

"I'm not."

"Oh, well your mom thinks you are. She's convinced

you're somehow dying. I thought she was going a little overboard, but then she said you called off work, and I had all sorts of crazy thoughts—cancer, heart attack, but then I just remembered it was early as fuck and I'd gotten woken up because you're suddenly a normal human being who doesn't go to work once in a while. Then, I just wanted to kill you. It'd be easier if you were dying on your own."

Miles gripped the phone tighter. "You're all mental. Every single one of you. I don't feel well. That's it." Was it really such a big deal that he didn't go in to work today? Apparently, it was. Quinn was right. He was boring.

"You're in a car. Why are you in a car, Miles?"

"I'm running away," he answered. He probably should. It was the only way they would leave him alone.

Chance sighed. "Seriously...you okay, boo? Does this have anything to do with what had you upset Friday night?"

Miles looked over at Quinn, who stared back at him. He considered playing it off, making up some kind of excuse, but then he remembered that he demanded honesty from everyone else. What right did he have if he didn't give it himself?

"I'm fine. I'm...going to the beach."

"You hate the beach," Chance replied.

Yeah, he usually did. He was looking forward to it today, though.

He risked another quick glance at Quinn whose brows were pulled together. Just as he thought. Quinn could hear Chance.

"I'm going with a friend," Miles admitted. Should he have

said boyfriend? Dude he was banging? Dating? They'd decided they were boyfriends.

"You hate friends…except us."

Fucking Chance. "I don't hate friends, you jackass. I'm driving so unless you really want me to die, I'm going to go." He paused, then added, "And I'm bringing someone to Wild Side on Friday."

"What? You're—"

"I'm hanging up now," Miles told him.

"Don't you end this call, Miles! You're bringing someone to Wild Side and going to the beach? Who are you and what did you do with my best friend? I—"

Miles hung up before Chance could continue.

"You hate the beach," Quinn said. "I mentioned the beach our first weekend and you said you didn't hate it."

It was then Miles realized that's why Quinn had chosen it. For him.

Miles looked at him and gave Quinn another truth. "I don't hate the beach today. With you." And it hadn't been as hard to say as Miles thought it would.

"We haven't gotten there yet."

"That part doesn't matter." Brutal fucking honesty.

THEY'D DECIDED TO go to Manhattan Beach. Well, Quinn had decided, since apparently Miles didn't even like the fucking beach, yet here Quinn was dragging him there right after they'd decided to be together and Quinn talked him out of going to work.

I don't hate the beach today. With you.

Okay, so that part had helped. Miles was here when he didn't do shit like this. He didn't call in to work. He'd thought it was an exaggeration until the man had gotten a phone call from both his mom and his best friend just because he stayed home.

There was something big going on between them. Quinn could feel it in every one of his nerve endings, in the marrow of his bones. Could feel it in the way his pulse sped up around Miles. He wouldn't mention it because Miles would likely spook. Plus, maybe he was overreacting, or maybe it just felt big and would fizzle out quickly.

Maybe he was afraid to jinx it.

To lose it.

Miles wasn't the only one who feared being left behind.

Quinn couldn't remember truly being scared of losing someone he cared about in a very long time.

Once Miles parked, they grabbed their bags out of the trunk and made their way down to the sand. It was only about ten thirty, but the sun was already bright and the beach was already coming to life. Surfers, joggers, and bicyclists had likely already been here for hours.

"Thanks for coming with me," Quinn said as they walked through the clean sand. Manhattan Beach was always nice.

"Apparently, I need it. I'm a little worried they'll send out a search party for me. Chance has a big mouth. I'm sure everyone knows I'm here by now, which means they'll think

I've been abducted. I hope you don't get arrested." Miles winked. Playful Miles was even sexier than serious Miles.

"You'll just have to defend me if they come looking for me...or I'll have to hide you away real good." Quinn was intrigued by the idea of hiding Miles away and keeping him to himself.

"I like the hiding idea."

"I was just thinking the same," Quinn replied.

They found a quieter stretch of beach and laid their blanket out.

Miles pulled his shirt over his head and Quinn watched the reveal. He took in the sight of Miles's dark brown skin, taut across his firm muscles. The ridges and dips in his abs and the hardness of his pecs and the tightness in his triceps when he moved.

"You keep looking at me like that and I won't be responsible for my actions." Miles tossed his tee to the blanket.

"You're gorgeous."

"So are you," he replied and then walked over. It was Miles who pulled Quinn's shirt off and Miles who grabbed the sunscreen from the bag. "I only want your skin red when it's from my hand," Miles told him as he rubbed the lotion into Quinn's shoulders, back, chest, and arms.

Quinn took the bottle back and returned the favor, smearing it into Miles's skin as well.

"Why did we leave the house again?" Quinn teased.

Miles winked at him. "You be real good and I'll make it up to you tonight."

"Right now?"

"Tonight."

"I suddenly feel like we switched places. I'm supposed to be the one who likes to go out while you want to stay home."

Miles chuckled and then pulled off his shorts, leaving him in only a pair of royal blue Speedos. He filled them out well, of course, his cock and balls making a nice bulge.

"At least I get to enjoy the view," Quinn told him.

"Get your shorts off so I can too."

Quinn wore a pair of tight, red swimming trunks that made his ass look nice.

Miles swatted it, just as a man walked by and chuckled at them.

"You keep your hands to yourself, Counselor. You're the one who said I have to wait until I get home."

"I changed my mind." Miles cocked a brow at Quinn, but Quinn backed away.

He wanted to play, so he said, "None of that. Race you to the water."

He ran and heard Miles curse before there were footsteps behind him. Quinn made it waist deep in the water before arms went around him, and they fell together, breaking the top of the water, laughing.

Miles was having fun. Quinn could see it in the light in his eyes and the tilt of his grin and Quinn was damn proud—not only to see it, but to have a part in putting the look on Miles's face.

Yeah, he wasn't exaggerating. This was something big and he, for one, couldn't be happier about it.

CHAPTER EIGHTEEN

T HEY PLAYED IN the water for quite a while. Miles couldn't remember the last time he'd actually enjoyed the ocean. Afterward, they joined a game of volleyball on the beach. Miles and Quinn had been on opposite teams, and Quinn's team had won—the fucker. Miles had insisted they play a second game, in which his team won, so he felt better after that.

After Miles redeemed himself, they grabbed a couple orders of French fries and were walking down the beach, which was much busier than it had been earlier.

"This is refreshing," Miles found himself saying. "I don't typically do things like this."

"No shit? I never would have known."

Miles shook his head. "Good point," he replied because obviously what Quinn said was true, and they both knew it.

"Have you always been a control freak?" Quinn asked.

"I resent that," Miles replied before saying, "Yes." Because he was and he always had been. There was no sense in denying it. "I must have driven Chance and Ollie crazy when we were younger. I was always the one organizing the games and deciding whose house we stayed at that weekend." He chuckled, thinking back. They'd had a lot of fun. He was lucky to have them. "I used to have this obsession with pacts. I'd make us have a pact about everything—our friendship, plans for the future, how we would approach the upcoming school year."

"You were afraid of being alone," Quinn said softly. "That they'd leave you behind?"

He sighed, popped a French fry into his mouth and realized, "Yeah, I guess I was. I guess I thought if there was some kind of rules, binding us together, they couldn't walk away." Fuck. That wasn't easy to admit. The thought made him sad at the same time. He shouldn't fear these things. He had so many people in his life who loved him.

"But they never did walk away and they never will. I bet they wouldn't have without Child Lawyer Miles legally binding them to him either."

He found himself laughing. He never thought he would laugh in a situation like this—realizing how insecure he'd always been. "No…no, I guess they wouldn't have. I'd write out contracts, and they'd sign them no matter how ridiculous they were."

"Oh fuck. It was worse than pacts? You really did go all child lawyer on them."

He sure had. "I'm lucky to have them."

"They're lucky to have you too," Quinn answered in return.

He shrugged because he wasn't so sure about that. "I think that's part of the reason I struggled so much with Matt.

Chance and Ollie? I knew them. I trusted them. Our parents were close. Then there was this kid who was suddenly a part of what had always been the three of us. Ollie had been in love with him from the start, and it scared the shit out of me. What if Matt took Oliver away? What if that was just the beginning, and I lost Chance too?" He rubbed a hand over his face. This was getting out of hand quickly. "Fuck. Okay, that's enough with that. Stop your damn voodoo magic, making me admit shit I don't like to admit." Even to himself.

"Change can be scary. It was for me. I never knew what to expect when I'd get placed in another home or orphanage. You were a kid. It makes sense. But the thing is, change doesn't always have to be bad. You were scared of losing Chance and Oliver but you didn't. All you did was gain someone else who cared about you in Matt." And now he'd gained someone in Quinn as well. Someone who'd rocked his fucking world in the most surprising way.

"So you're telling me I was an asshole for nothing?" he teased.

"Nope. It's always smart to try to protect yourself. I learned that lesson the hard way, but you can't protect yourself to the point where you're missing out on the good stuff too. Take me for example. You tried to push me away and now you can't imagine your life without me." There was a light, playful tone to Quinn's voice.

"I wouldn't go that far…"

"Of course you wouldn't, Counselor." They passed a trash can and Quinn tossed his remaining French fries in it and then threaded his arm through Miles's.

He wanted to know how Quinn hadn't protected himself. He wanted to know the details about why Quinn couldn't sleep at night.

He wanted to know every fucking thing about him that he could.

And damn it, he wanted Quinn to know all his dark places too. Wanted Quinn to explore parts of him that no one had seen—not Ollie or Chance or Matt. Hell, maybe not even himself. "I—"

"Oh!" Quinn cut him off. "We have to go get lemon cupcakes. They have the best lemon cupcakes you will ever eat."

Before Miles could reply, Quinn was dragging him to the shop where they would apparently get lemon cupcakes.

They were so different, he and Quinn. But they somehow fit. Quinn brought a fullness to his chest he wasn't sure he'd ever had.

As they waited in line for what must be popular cupcakes, Quinn faced him, dropped his voice low. "I have another question for you."

The fact that he warned Miles ahead of time, told him Quinn's question was a serious one. "Okay…"

"Have you ever thought about trying to find them? You have the means…and the resources…" Miles was a lawyer as was his dad. They'd have a good chance at finding his biological parents.

"No," Miles answered sharply then sighed because they were having a good day, and he didn't want to be a dickhead.

He put his arms around Quinn and pulled him close. "I don't want to talk about that. I want to talk about lemon cupcakes."

As silence stretched on before Quinn replied, Miles thought he might keep it going. Might ask more questions, but eventually, he just asked, "You do, huh?"

"Yep."

"Okay, we can do that. They're like little bites of orgasmic heaven," Quinn said, and Miles laughed. They got their cupcakes and then made their way back to their spot on the beach.

"These are good," Miles said. He was about to lick the frosting off his finger when Quinn grabbed his wrist and did it for him.

"That was mine," he said with a smile.

"It's mine now." Quinn winked and lay down. God, he was ridiculous.

Miles's phone went off. He grabbed it and saw an email from work. "Let me reply to this real quick." Before he could, the phone was jerked out of his hand.

"No work today."

"Give me my phone back," he told Quinn.

"No. You can work later. Right now, you're hanging out with me." Quinn stuffed the phone under his towel and then lay down, using his towel for a pillow.

"I hate you," Miles told him as he fought off a smile.

"No you don't." Quinn closed his eyes. Miles watched him for a moment, and when it became clear he wasn't going to open them again, he lay down beside him. It wasn't long before Quinn rolled over onto his stomach and it was obvious, he'd fallen asleep.

Miles could get his phone back. He could slip his hand under the towel and take it, but for some reason, he didn't.

He closed his eyes for a while and rested. He didn't fall asleep the way Quinn did but he relaxed.

He didn't know how much time had passed when he opened his eyes, rolled to his side, and propped his head up in his hand while resting on his elbow and looking down at Quinn.

He examined the freckles dotting Quinn's upper back and shoulders. Miles's eyes traveled down to his lean waist and tight ass. How the hell had they gotten here? And why did Miles like this place he was in so much—this space with Quinn.

He was…surprising. Unexpected. In the short time they'd known each other, he'd burrowed his way inside Miles, past all those defenses he hadn't set on purpose but were there nonetheless. The same way Quinn was now inside of him too.

He figured it had been a good two hours since they lay down. Quinn's shoulders were a slight pink, and Miles found himself leaning closer. Letting his fingers dance along Quinn's skin.

He kissed one freckle, and then another. "Wake up, baby boy. You're going to burn."

Quinn groaned but didn't open his eyes. "Mmm. Do that again."

"What? This?" Miles asked before kissing Quinn's shoulder

again.

"Yep," he said in a rough, sleepy voice, so Miles did. He peppered soft kisses all along Quinn's skin. He felt like a different man, here with Quinn. Like he'd been released from binds he always kept himself in.

"Thank you," he whispered before touching his lips to Quinn's flesh again.

"What are you thanking me for?"

Without looking, he knew then that Quinn had opened his eyes. "For making me call off work. For dragging me here. For...I don't know. Everything."

Quinn moved, so Miles tilted his head back to give him space to roll over. When he did, they were eye to eye. "You don't have anything to thank me for. There's nowhere else I want to be right now."

There was nowhere else Miles wanted to be either.

He leaned down at that, teased Quinn's mouth with his tongue and then kissed him deeply. Tasted lemon and thought it was somehow sweeter coming from Quinn.

Maybe Quinn didn't think Miles had anything to thank him for, but he did.

CHAPTER NINETEEN

Q UINN WAS ACTUALLY nervous.

It wasn't often that many things affected him like this, but it was more because of Miles than himself. Miles was stepping outside of his comfort zone. He was pulling Quinn further into his life, introducing him to the people who meant the most to him, and Quinn didn't take that lightly.

He didn't take any of what was going on between himself and Miles lightly.

"Fuck," he gritted out as he looked through his closet to find something to wear.

He'd come to his apartment after work today. He'd spent a few nights this week with Miles. It was strange, becoming used to sleeping in another bed with someone again the way he used to do with Christian—only with Miles, he was naked and there was touching and spanking and coming.

Quinn was falling for him. There was no doubt about that and it was strange and exciting and maybe scary as fuck, too, because it was so new for him. And as new as it was for Quinn, it would be even more so for Miles.

He grabbed a powder blue V-neck shirt from his closet. He'd just gotten out of the shower and cleaned up.

He'd just pulled the shirt over his head and dragged a pair of short, blue, mesh trunks on when the doorbell rang.

One glance at the clock told him Miles was early.

He didn't know why but that made him smile.

Quinn walked into the living room and pulled the door open. Miles was...fuck, he was gorgeous wearing a white, button-up shirt, the top three buttons left open, and black jeans.

He hadn't shaved—dark stubble along his strong jawline.

His eyes scanned Quinn up and down, and Quinn saw the hunger there, the desire. It made his cock perk up and his body flush hot.

"You don't look so bad yourself," he told Miles.

"I didn't say you looked good."

Quinn winked. "You didn't have to. So I should skip the pants?"

Miles walked inside, grabbed Quinn's ass and pulled Quinn flush against him. "Only if you don't plan on leaving this apartment."

"No. No way, big guy. I'm not letting you try to sex-talk me out of going to meet your friends. I'm going even if you don't." He pushed Miles's hands away and went back toward his room.

"I'm going. I don't cancel Wild Side."

No, he wouldn't, would he? He would feel as though he was letting his friends down. He was so damn noble and loyal. Did he know it, Quinn wondered? And as much as he loved that about Miles...there was a small part of him that was jealous too.

He wanted to be that important to Miles, he realized. It wasn't as though he would ever expect to mean to him what his friends did or to take their place, but he wanted his own important spot in Miles's life, as well. A spot that was carved out for him, and him alone.

"What's wrong?" Miles asked as he stepped into the bedroom behind Quinn. He looked up to discover he could see Miles's reflection in the mirror, which was how Miles had seen his face.

"Nothing's wrong, Counselor. I'm fine." He was. He had no reason not to be.

"You looked a little sad all of a sudden." Miles stepped up behind him, wrapped his arms around Quinn's waist, and lowered his mouth to Quinn's ear. "When I made the comment about staying, I wasn't trying to get out of going to Wild Side. I want…I want you to meet my friends."

He was so goddamn sweet and sentimental and he didn't even know it. The way those words and that knowledge made Quinn's chest swell. "You have a good heart, Miles. You love big. Your friends are lucky to have you."

"Nah." He shook his head. "You caught me on a bad day." Miles stepped back and swatted Quinn's ass. "Oh, I really like these underwear. Get dressed before I pull them under your cheeks and spend the next few hours with my tongue in your ass."

"Promises, promises." Quinn winked but then went and did exactly what Miles said.

Wild Side first, tongue in ass later.

———— ∿ ————

MILES WAS NERVOUS.

It was fucking ridiculous, and he was fully aware of that, but he was, and he thought maybe Quinn felt the same.

He was making things official with Quinn. He was entwining the other man in his life when he'd never done that with another living soul.

He'd been angry with Oliver when he tried to do it with Matt, and now it was his turn.

"Is it okay to admit I'm scared?" Quinn asked after they parked and began walking toward Wild Side. It was familiar as breathing—the busy street and the sign with the silver W with a circle around it.

"Why would you be scared?" he questioned.

"Oh, I don't know. Maybe because they're important to you. Because you love them, and I kind of like you so I really want them to like me."

He stopped at that. Felt a wild gallop in his chest. Christ, this man turned him inside out. He put a finger beneath Quinn's chin and lifted his head. "You only kind of like me?"

"Sometimes. I forgot the sometimes. Other times you drive me fucking crazy." He grinned and Miles leaned in and pressed a quick kiss to his lips. His admission that Quinn was nervous—that he cared this much what Chance, Matt, and Ollie thought about him—was exactly what he needed to hear. It made a calmness ease through his veins. Made his muscles relax in ways they hadn't for hours.

"They'll like you. I know they will." How could someone not like Quinn? And the truth was, they would love Quinn because he was important to Miles. Jesus, he'd somehow become a necessity.

"Aw, shucks. Thanks." Quinn's brows pulled together. "Did you say that so you can get in my pants?"

"Please. Like you wouldn't let me in your pants."

"Oh, I see Cocky Miles is back."

"Cocky Miles never went anywhere, baby boy." Miles winked.

"Fuck, that was sexy."

"Let's go inside before we don't make it." They stood in the line, which moved quickly. Miles put a hand at the small of Quinn's back as they made their way through the loud, packed bar. Quinn obviously knew where they sat, since he'd seen Miles here one night, but he let Miles lead the way.

The second they stepped up to the table, six eyes shot up at them and held fast.

Oliver smiled.

Chance cocked a brow.

Matt looked…fuck, he almost looked proud. And like a light bulb clicked into place because he likely recognized Quinn from the night they'd seen him here. Chance and Oliver probably recognized him too, but they didn't show it.

"Oh, you're gorgeous. What are you doing with Miles?" Chance broke the ice.

"Fuck off," Miles gritted out.

"When you're done with him, call me." Chance held his hand to his ear like a phone and Quinn laughed.

Fucking Chance. He felt like he was always saying that.

"I like you. I think we're going to be friends. I'm Quinn." He held out his hand and Chance shook it.

"Chance. Nice to meet you."

Quinn reached out to Oliver next. Then Matt. Miles took the seat beside Matt, and Quinn beside him, between himself and Chance.

"Holy shit. I almost don't know what to think. There's new blood at the West Hollywood Boys' table!" Dare, the bar owner, stepped up to the table and crossed his arms. "You look familiar."

"I've been here once before. I'm Quinn."

"I knew it!" Chance said between fake coughs. They all ignored him.

"Nice to meet you," Dare replied. "I'll grab you guys some drinks. What do you want?"

They put in an order—Miles and Quinn both getting Jack and Coke before Dare disappeared through the crowd.

"West Hollywood Boys, huh? You're like the 'it' guys here. You know I'm gonna tease you about that, right? Tell me you know it." Quinn grinned at Miles who rolled his eyes.

"You tease me about everything."

"That's because it's fun to see you get so ruffled."

"I hate you," Miles teased.

"No you don't, Counselor. I already know you like me."

"You like me too."

"Yeah but you like me more," Quinn echoed.

Miles chuckled and Quinn winked. When he looked up, he realized his friends were staring at them, eyes wide and jaws slack.

Chance even pinched himself.

Oh fuck, this was going to be a ridiculous night. Yes, he was dating. It was different. He got it. They better not make a big deal out of it. "If you guys stare at me like that, we're leaving."

"Quinn and Miles…" Chance said to the tune of the kid's song that would next have them in a tree.

"How old are you?" Miles asked him.

"Oh. I'm sorry. I'll be good since your boyfriend is here." Chance winked at Quinn.

"Don't be good on my behalf," Quinn replied and Miles realized he was fucking in for it tonight. Quinn and Chance together definitely would be relentless…and Matt and Ollie? They'd just look at him like they knew some secret Miles hadn't figured out yet.

Why didn't that thought bother him more than it did?

CHAPTER TWENTY

"WOW. THAT'S REALLY fantastic what you do, Austin. I'd love to jump in and help any way I can," Quinn told the redhead. Austin and Dare had joined them a little while ago. It wasn't something they never did, which made the fact that Miles had freaked out about it the other night even worse.

"We're always looking for volunteers. Oliver helps out," Austin told Quinn, and Miles watched as Quinn made eye contact with Ollie. He wanted this, Miles could tell.

"Yeah. It's great. The kids are really wonderful. It's become a very important part of my life," Ollie replied. "I can get your number from Miles, and maybe we can set something up."

Miles felt Quinn tense up slightly and he knew what it was for. Quinn wasn't sure how Miles would feel about that. If Miles would turn into an asshole on him again.

He'd definitely connected with Miles's friends tonight but Miles had noticed he tread the line very carefully, obviously worried that Miles would feel he encroached on his life, which made him a dickhead. Quinn shouldn't have to be so careful.

Miles wrapped an arm around Quinn's shoulders. "I'll text you his number," Miles told Oliver. The words stuck in his throat slightly but Miles ignored it.

Quinn relaxed, touched his leg, and Miles welcomed the feel of his hand there.

"I grew up in the system," Quinn announced. "I bounced around from home to home most of my life. It'd feel good to help kids who are struggling, too. Oh. You know what we can do? Maybe we can set up something at my work? They can come in and test some of the games. Or if that wouldn't work, I can arrange to have equipment brought to the center. It'll take some finagling but I can make it happen. Do you think they would like something like that?"

Austin's eyes practically glowed.

Oliver cocked his head, studied Miles and Quinn, but none of that mattered to Miles right then. Nothing mattered other than Quinn. Miles's pulse jackhammered and his chest began to ache, to feel a fullness that made it almost impossible to breathe.

"Wow…that's incredible, Quinn," Austin answered. "They would love it. Dare spent some time on the streets when he was a teenager, so I'm sure he can relate to how that felt. If you don't mind, I'll get your number from Miles as well. We can set up a meeting to see what we can figure out."

Miles nodded but didn't look away from Quinn. He hadn't known that about Dare. He also didn't know why Quinn's offer struck him so deep in his chest, but it did. It wasn't just that either. Wasn't just Quinn's kindness when it came to helping kids or the way he could announce his past so easily…it was seeing him fit so seamlessly with Chance, Matt, and Oliver. It was seeing his worlds combined in a way he never thought. Hell, he never pictured much of a world for himself outside of his job, his parents, and his friends, but here Quinn was becoming this whole new universe for Miles to explore.

"Of course. Go for it," Quinn answered Austin, but then glanced toward Miles. He could see the wheels turning in Quinn's brain. Could see that Quinn knew this night meant something to Miles, meant more to him than he thought it would.

Quinn winked then turned away, giving Miles space, but he didn't think he needed it. He really fucking didn't. Space was the last thing he wanted from Quinn right now.

"You have an eyelash on your face." Chance reached out and collected the lash from Quinn's cheek. That was strangely his thing but unlike he'd do with Miles, he moved to wipe it away when Quinn stopped him.

"What the fuck are you doing? I have to make a wish," Quinn said.

An ear-to-ear smile pulled across Chance's face. "I love you. Like, I really think I'm in love with you. Miles acts like I'm torturing him when I force him to make a wish."

Chance's eyes were lined in black. He winked at Miles who shook his head. "I'm not *that* bad."

"You don't like wishes? It's as though I don't even know you anymore…" Quinn teased, and the whole table erupted in laughter.

At his expense, of course.

"I hate you all," he said but really he thought it might be the best Friday night he'd ever had.

⁓

THEY WERE BOTH quiet on the way home.

Quinn didn't know what Miles was thinking, but it was pretty obvious he had something on his mind.

Quinn did as well.

Their relationship had taken a turn tonight. At least on Quinn's side. Sitting at the table at Wild Side, he'd felt part of a group, felt a friendship and camaraderie that he wasn't sure he'd ever experienced. Yes, he had friends and coworkers and Christian. He laughed with people and drank with people and went out with people, but it was very rare that there was a connection he felt in his bones. A mutual respect and passion that he'd lived tonight. That he felt with Miles every day and he now felt with Miles's friends.

They were a group who loved each other fiercely. Who cared about others. Who had accepted him into their fold because he was with Miles. It wasn't often people found that kind of relationship, that soul-deep connection, and Quinn wasn't sure why it almost made him feel…sad.

Maybe the sorrow came from not knowing exactly how Miles felt about tonight and if things would change between them. If he would run or pull back, because Quinn was getting too close, or if he'd hold tight.

Quinn wanted to hold tight…but he needed Miles to do that, too.

They were heading toward Quinn's place and not Miles's, which he wasn't sure was a very good sign.

When they arrived home, Miles pulled into a parking spot and asked, "Can I come up?"

"Yeah, yeah, of course you can," Quinn replied. To talk or stay, Quinn didn't know.

"I need to shower," Quinn told Miles after they were closed up in his place.

"Okay, I'll be out here."

Quinn frowned but didn't argue. Miles typically never passed up the chance to see him naked, which didn't bode well.

Without another word, Quinn walked out of the room. He got his shower started and stripped out of his clothes, suddenly disappointed Miles didn't get to take his sexy, new trunks off him.

He washed his body, then hair, before savoring the hot spray beating down on his skin. He thought about tonight— about laughing and talking and bonding with Miles and his friends.

Quinn wanted to be there with them every Friday night, he realized. Wanted to see Miles roll his eyes at Chance while knowing Miles loved him more than anything. Wanted to hear him tease Oliver about being all heart and ask Matt about his music and know that there wasn't anything in the world that Miles wouldn't do for those men. It took someone special to love like that. He thought maybe he wanted Miles to love him that way as well.

He sighed then turned off the water. The second he stepped out of the shower, his eyes snagged with Miles's, who stood in the doorway, leaning against the jamb with his arms crossed.

"I've never felt anything like the way tonight made me feel." Miles's voice was all raw, bare-bones honesty. "Seeing you with them…with my friends. Hearing you laugh with them and fit in with them and…" He shook his head as though he didn't know what else to say.

Quinn's heart damn near jumped out of his chest, it beat so proudly. "Yeah, I felt it too. It was like…I don't know. Like I fit, but I didn't know if it was just something I wanted too damn badly that I imagined it or if it was real."

"It was real," Miles replied.

Thank God. "Okay, next thought. I didn't know what you'd think about my fitting in." Water ran down his body. A strand of wet hair fell against his right brow as he held his breath and waited for Miles to answer.

"I didn't know what I would think about it either."

"Do you know now?" Quinn asked.

"It was…" Miles shrugged. He was contemplative and unsure, but somehow still the strong, dominant force who took Quinn's breath away. Maybe the combination took his breath away even more.

"It was what, Counselor? Brutal honesty, remember?" Quinn probed.

"It was everything." The moment the last syllable left Miles's lips, the two men were moving toward each other.

Quinn almost slipped on the wet floor, but Miles grabbed his biceps, holding him up. Their mouths crashed together, their tongues diving, seeking, searching.

Miles's hands went to Quinn's bare ass. He stumbled backward, walked backward, holding both himself and Quinn up.

They made it to the middle of Quinn's room, clawing and kissing and trying to climb inside each other's skin.

"Get on your knees for me, baby boy. I want to see my cock stretching those pretty lips of yours."

Quinn's fucking pleasure. He loved sucking Miles's dick.

Quinn kissed Miles's throat, worked his buttons, and then shoved the shirt off his shoulders, revealing all that taut, creamy-brown skin.

He kissed Miles's chest.

Licked it.

His abs.

Then dropped to his knees and worked the button on his jeans with shaky fingers.

"I've never wanted anyone so much," Quinn admitted as he unzipped Miles's pants then shoved them down.

He wore a pair of tight, royal blue trunks that looked so fucking delicious against his dark skin.

Miles's hand tangled in the back of his hair. He pushed Quinn against his bulge, made him nuzzle it, which Quinn savored every second of.

"Yeah, me either," Miles admitted. "Take me out. Need to feel that hot mouth of yours."

Quinn jerked Miles's underwear down, licked his lips as Miles's dick popped free. Jesus, he was fucking big—long and thick and leaking. Quinn lashed his tongue over the drop at his slit, then sucked the fat head of Miles's erection between his lips.

He wanted to devour him. To suck him until he came down his throat.

"Fuck yes. So good, baby boy. You feel so fucking good." Miles thrust his hips slightly, not too much, but enough to work his way deeper into Quinn's mouth.

Quinn looked up at him, pulled off and said, "I guess this gag will work as well as anything else," before sucking Miles deep again.

His own cock ached, throbbed it was so damn hard.

"That's it. Just like that. Christ, you look so fucking gorgeous down there. Put your hands behind your back. Pretend I have them tied there."

Lust rolled through Quinn's body. God, this man knew how to get him amped up. He wished Miles did have him tied up, tied down to do whatever he wanted to Quinn.

He did as Miles said, keeping his hands behind his back as though they were cuffed there, while he sat on his knees and blew Miles.

Miles's hand was in his hair. He slid it over to cup Quinn's face and brushed his thumb over Quinn's cheek.

"You make me fucking crazy. Like you fit into this empty space I didn't know I had."

"Me too," Quinn admitted before moving down to nuzzle

Miles's full, heavy sac.

His arms fell away.

"No. I didn't say you could move those. Put them back. You don't need anything more than your mouth right now."

No, no he didn't. Quinn positioned his hands again, ran his tongue to the tip of Miles's cock, then sucked him again.

Miles's breathing picked up and the movements of his hips got sharper. Just when Quinn thought he couldn't take it anymore—when he thought he'd go crazy if he didn't get to taste Miles before Miles took his turn with Quinn—Miles jerked back, pulled Quinn to his feet and practically growled at him. "My turn. Lie on your belly. It's about time I got to taste that hole I love so fucking much."

Quinn damn near came right there.

CHAPTER TWENTY-ONE

MILES DIDN'T FEEL like himself. It was as though being with Quinn made him a different man. A better man.

His body buzzed, came alive in ways he couldn't hold in. Like he would burst apart at the seams, and he didn't mind going that way. Didn't mind opening himself up to Quinn because it felt…right. Felt good in a way nothing had before— not even Chance, Oliver, and Matt.

Quinn lay in the middle of the bed, ass there waiting for him. Miles climbed between his spread legs. Rubbed his hand down Quinn's back and over his butt, watching his guy shudder as he did.

That's who Quinn was—at least for him. He was *his* and Miles would savor that.

He swatted one of Quinn's cheeks. Watched him writhe and heard him groan and then did the same to the other.

Quinn pushed his ass back, close to Miles, but Miles put a hand on the small of his back. "No, just lie there for me. I'll do you right."

Quinn relaxed, doing just as Miles said, so he swatted Quinn's ass again. Then again and again and again until his cheeks were such a gorgeous fucking pink.

"What's it feel like?" Miles asked. He'd never been on the receiving end, and didn't really want to be, but he wanted to know what it was like for Quinn. Wanted to be sure he was giving this man everything he needed.

"It stings...so fucking good. Heat rushes through me each time your hand hits my skin."

Miles smacked his ass again, wanting to give Quinn more of that sting.

"Fuck yes... It's... God, such a delicious fucking burn. It starts off like a spark and then just ignites—fire and pleasure shooting through me."

That's what Miles wanted to hear. It's what he wanted Quinn to feel.

"I know, baby boy." He rubbed Quinn's shoulders. "I love these...all these little freckles." He'd told Quinn that before, hadn't he? Miles didn't care. He'd tell him a hundred more times.

"I thought you were gonna put your tongue in me?"

Miles smiled. "I thought I was in charge?"

"Please?"

"I like it when you beg."

"Do it now." Quinn wiggled his red ass, and Miles couldn't hold himself back. He lay down, between Quinn's legs, spread his cheeks, and took in his tight, pink hole.

"So fucking perfect." He rubbed it with his thumb. And then he dove in, flicking his tongue back and forth over Quinn's pucker. Burying his face between Quinn's flushed cheeks.

There was nothing in the world he loved more than ass, and he tried to show Quinn that. Make him feel it with each lick, with each probe of his finger and his tongue in Quinn's tight hole.

Quinn thrust his ass back, tried to ride Miles's face.

"Patience," Miles told him.

"I want to come."

"You will." He dove in again. Bit Quinn's ass cheek, licked and ate at his rim. Smiled against his flesh as Quinn writhed beneath him until he almost lost his own damn mind in the process.

He pulled back, lay on Quinn's back, and licked the shell of his ear. "Do you want a chance at my ass tonight?" He needed to give Quinn what he wanted tonight, whatever it was, because Quinn had given him something, even if he didn't realize it.

"No…" Quinn rushed out breathlessly. "Want your dick. Thank you, though."

And Miles would give it to him.

He leaned forward, grabbed the condom and lube from the drawer and suited up. He squirted cold lube into his hand, and stroked his aching cock.

"Lie on your side," he told Quinn who obeyed. Miles lay behind him, on his side as well. Quinn bent his top leg and pushed it forward, giving Miles access to his ass.

Miles squirted more lube into his hand, rubbed it on Quinn's rim, then pushed the head of his cock inside all that tight fucking heat.

"Oh fuck." His eyes rolled back like he'd never been inside Quinn before.

Quinn trembled, seemed to melt into the fucking mattress. "More," he begged and Miles gave it to him, pushed in balls deep. He wrapped his arm around Quinn, kissed his shoulder as he rutted into him from behind.

Miles took him slowly, worked him real fucking good, as he kept peppering kisses to his shoulders. "Goddamn, this hole. Best I ever had," he whispered in Quinn's ear as he made love to him.

"God," Quinn said and Miles thrust.

"Yes," Quinn added as Miles pulled out.

Miles pumped his hips, played with Quinn's nipple, ran his hand up his pecs, squeezed them just needing to touch Quinn everywhere.

He wanted to look at him too.

"Ride me," Miles said then pulled out and rolled to his back. Quinn was there immediately, straddling him.

Miles held the base of his cock, lined it up with Quinn's hole as his guy lowered onto it. He rolled his hips, fucking himself on Miles's prick.

Jesus, he knew how to work that ass.

Miles grabbed his hips, dug his fingers in.

"God I love being all up in you."

Quinn looked down at him, with a crooked, cocky grin and dimples. "That's because I'm good."

"Tell me you want me inside of you too."

"I always want your cock in my ass." He leaned forward

and kissed Miles. Their tongues tangled and Miles thrust inside him. His balls were so goddamned full, ached so fucking much.

He wrapped his hand around Quinn's dick, jacked him as Quinn rode him, as his tight ass fisted Miles's cock.

When Quinn spurted, he shot his hot load all over Miles's hand. Miles let himself fall too, let his orgasm skyrocket through him as he emptied his load in the condom.

Quinn fell on top of him, breathing heavily in his ear, and as Miles ran his hands up and down Quinn's sweaty back, he realized he was in love with him. That for the first time in his life, he loved. Someone had penetrated the walls he kept around himself and Miles wanted the other man there. Wanted Quinn to burrow inside him as deeply as he could.

That he never wanted to let Quinn go.

He wrapped his arms around Quinn tightly, breathed him in—the scent of sweat and sex and Quinn. "Will you tell me?" Miles asked, somehow knowing Quinn would know what he meant.

"Yeah." Quinn leaned away from him, pulled the condom off Miles's softening dick, and tossed it into the trash, before lying on top of him again.

Miles's arms went around him a second time, holding him and skating his fingers up and down Quinn's spine.

Quinn kissed his neck. Licked his collarbone before settling in. "I was between homes. I was close to aging out. Who the fuck wants an almost-seventeen-year-old kid?"

"Everyone should want you."

"Aw, you're sweet." Quinn winked but Miles was serious.

"Anyway, I had this friend," Quinn continued. "His name was Kane. We hit it off—had each other's backs. There were some fucked-up people in the group home—fights and shit. Bad crew."

Miles tightened his hold, wished he had been there to protect Quinn.

"They took a liking to us, which means they liked to fuck with us. We'd sleep in shifts, ya know? Watching out for each other. He was the only person I trusted enough to watch me while I slept."

Miles closed his eyes, not liking where this was going.

"So, it was my turn to stay awake. I was fucking tired. I don't know what in the hell was going on with me. I was usually good at staying awake when I needed to." He stopped, took a deep breath and Miles felt the pain through his breathing. In the way his body moved and he turned away.

Miles grabbed Quinn's chin and turned his face so he looked at him. "Don't look away from me. This is me. You can tell me anything."

Quinn nodded, turned and kissed Miles's hand. That gentle touch made fire burn through his chest. Made his heart beat so fucking hard he didn't know if he could contain it.

"I guess you can figure out what happened from there. I fell asleep. They started beating the shit out of us—starting with Kane because they knew he was the weakest out of the two of us. They hurt him horribly."

Quinn closed his eyes, and Miles said, "It wasn't your

fault," because he knew Quinn blamed himself. It was the kind of man he was.

"Wasn't it, though?"

"No, baby. It wasn't. Were you the one who made them hurt you? No. That's on them. You just did what you had to do to survive. Blame them, not yourself. What happened afterward?" He ran his hands through Quinn's hair. Held him. Wanted to fucking kill anyone who had ever put their hands on him. Wanted to wrap him up in a bubble so no one could ever touch him again.

"Kane spent a few days in the hospital. I was fucked up pretty badly, but a trip to the ER was enough. Ever since, I go through little phases where I can't sleep very well. I wake up thinking about what happened, or I'm afraid to close my eyes, even though I know no one will hurt me... And I'm also cautious on who I sleep with. Fucking is one thing, sleeping is another. I used to stay with Christian most of the time. He was my best friend and it made it easy."

Miles felt a growl rise up inside of him at the thought of Quinn in bed with anyone else. "You ever struggle, you come to me. No one else. Even if..."

"You breaking up with me already?"

Miles didn't take the bait. "Say it. Say you'll come to me."

Quinn smiled and it damn near stopped Miles's heart. "I'll come to you."

"What happened to him? To Kane?"

"Kane said he didn't blame me. But that was it for our friendship. It was too painful for him. He went to another home, and I never saw him again, and ever since then, I've always wondered where he is… He was hurt because of me, Miles."

"No, he wasn't. And you were hurt too. I'd fucking kill them if I knew who it was." And he would.

"Aw, you want to protect my honor?" Quinn teased.

"That's not the only thing I want to do with you, but yes. I do."

"This is it, isn't it? This is the thing that's going to make you fall in love with me?" Quinn winked. His words were playful, but the feeling in Miles's chest? The need for this man? It was anything but a joke.

"Already there. Realized it earlier tonight. Didn't ever think that would happen for me, and I'm not real sure what to do about it." Those words weren't as hard to speak as he thought they would be.

"You're serious?" Quinn asked, awe in his voice. "You're really fucking serious?" His brows pulled together and he didn't turn away from Miles.

"Do you think I would lie about something like that? We should have known. You wouldn't have been at Wild Side with me tonight if that wasn't the case."

Quinn ran his hand over Miles's head, cupped his cheek. "Christ, you're incredible. You think you're not good at this stuff, but you are. You think you're so damn hard and you're so detached but you're not. You're all heart, Counselor, and I am so fucking in love with you too."

Pride welled up in Miles, like nothing he'd ever experienced before. It was like he could fucking fly. Like he could conquer the world and nothing could ever touch him. "That's good. Otherwise, I'd have to beat your tight little ass until you changed your mind." But then—

"Don't." Quinn cut him off, somehow sensing Miles's chain of thought. "I can see the wheels turning in there. I can see it in your eyes. One thing has nothing to do with the other. This isn't fiction where there has to be some deep reason for why we like the things we like. I need rough sex and being dominated because that's my kink, the same way it's yours. There's no other reason behind it. It has nothing to do with what happened, and if you change the way you treat me when we fuck, we're going to have a problem."

Miles smiled, squeezed him. "How did you know I was thinking that?"

"Goes back to that big-ass heart I was talking about." Quinn grinned. Nuzzled Miles's neck. "We're in love. Holy fuck. How did that happen?"

Yeah, they were in love. Go fucking figure. "Must be because of my dick. It's a miracle worker."

Miles flipped them so Quinn was on his back and he lay on top. Quinn's legs dropped open, making space for him.

"It's definitely not your sparkling personality," Quinn said.

This time, it was Miles's turn to nuzzle Quinn's neck. He was being cheesy and giddy and he was pretty sure he had a personality transplant, but he didn't care. "You're being very fucking naughty, *boy*. What am I going to do with you?"

"Punish me?" Quinn asked.

Yeah, he could do that. He'd love him, too.

CHAPTER TWENTY-TWO

"ARE YOU ALONE?" Chance asked into the phone and Miles rolled his eyes. It was Sunday morning. Quinn had stayed at his place both Friday and Saturday night, but he'd had some things to take care of so he had left this morning.

It had been…nice the past couple days. They'd basically done the same things they'd done the week before—laughed and talked and fucked, but now it was somehow different. Everything felt heavier now. Not heavy in an uncomfortable way, but more important. As though every interaction meant a little more and had more meat to it.

He was officially losing his mind. He'd just thought their interactions were meaty and not talking about dick or ass either.

Christ, what the fuck was the man doing to him?

Changing you.

"You're not alone, are you?" Chance asked again when Miles didn't answer. He figured he better answer before Chance alerted the chain of command that something could be wrong.

"You're ridiculous. And you sound ridiculous. Yes, I'm

alone, you dork."

"We're downstairs. We'll be right up!" Chance replied in a high-pitched, excited voice.

"What—" The line went dead before Miles could reply but he wasn't the least bit surprised. His fucking friends. He was going to kill them. There was no doubt in his mind what this little ambush was about.

Quinn.

He didn't get off the couch, and a couple minutes later, his door pushed open and what sounded like a herd of elephants trampled in.

"You have a motherfucking boyfriend!" Was the first thing out of Chance's mouth.

Miles rolled his eyes.

But he did, in fact, have a boyfriend.

"I can't believe you're taking part in this, Ollie," Miles replied as his three friends walked into the room. "You either, Matt."

"So you only expect this out of me?" Chance asked, but before Miles could jump in, Oliver spoke.

"Are you going to pretend you wouldn't do the same thing if it was one of us? I seem to remember you dragging me out of Wild Side and to Chance's apartment."

Shit. He'd hoped Oliver wouldn't bring that up. "Not the same thing," Miles lied.

"Of course it's not, because this is you." Matt winked and then sat beside him.

"You have a fucking boyfriend!" Chance said again before

sitting on the coffee table in front of Miles. Oliver took the seat on the other side of him. Fuckers. They were boxing him in—poised for attack at any moment.

"Was this part of the plan? Not leaving me an escape route?" There was no doubt in Miles's mind that it was.

"Of course." Chance winked. He had purple eyeliner on today and matching nail polish.

Miles sighed…thought about lying but the thing was, he didn't feel like it. He didn't want to lie about what Quinn was to him. The way he'd burrowed his own place into Miles's heart. He sure as shit didn't want to lie to his best friends about Quinn.

"Yes, I have a…boyfriend and I'll one-up you and admit that I love him. How's that for honesty?" He'd knocked them for a loop, which was exactly his plan…that and being honest about who Quinn was to him. It was important to Miles.

The room went so quiet, you could have heard a pin drop. The only sound he heard was a soft gasp from Oliver. The couch rustled under Matt when he adjusted his position. Miles waited. This wouldn't last long—not with his crew. He knew it would come in three…two…one… "Oh my fucking God! Miles! Where are you?" Chance jumped to his feet. "I'll find you! I promise. I don't believe this imposter for one moment!" He walked over and opened the pantry and stuck his head inside. "Miles, are you in there? Or did they take you to their planet?"

Motherfucker. Miles chuckled. Both Oliver and Matt joined him.

God, he loved them. He was so lucky to have these people in his life. "Get your ass over here," Miles told him.

"You may look like my Miles, but I know you're not him. See? I told you guys aliens were real and they have Miles." Chance walked back over to them, winked and then sat on the table again. "I'm giving you hell. I called that shit on the way over here. Hell, I called it Friday night, remember? I just never thought you'd admit it."

Miles rubbed a hand over his face. "I never thought I'd feel it." But he did. He really fucking did.

"Does he know?" Matt asked softly.

"Yeah… I told him Friday night."

"Wow. This is legit," Chance said.

"This is serious, Chance," Oliver replied, then looked at Miles. "You're different."

He was different. Miles couldn't deny that even if he wanted to…and he didn't. There wasn't a part of him that wanted to brush this under the rug or pretend it wasn't happening. "I'm happy." He shrugged. "I just…he fucking found his way in. I don't know how it happened but it did. He just…"

"Can't always put it into words, can you?" Matt asked. "For me, loving Ollie was always there, dormant I think, if only because I wasn't ready. Then it was just…too big to ignore or explain."

"Yeah." Miles looked at him. "Yeah, it is too big to explain." Because he realized then, that it was important as hell, he added, "I'm sorry."

"You have nothing to apologize to me for," Matt replied.

"But I do. I wasn't always fair to you. That was always my issue and not yours. I'm sorry about that." He thought maybe he and Matt had more in common than they realized. They were both afraid to love, to trust, afraid of getting hurt.

"It's okay." Matt smiled and Miles felt Oliver's hand on his shoulder, squeezing in silent support.

"It's like you're all grown up," Chance said.

"When are you planning on doing that?" Miles teased.

Chance winked. "Never."

"I take it he feels the same?" Oliver asked. He wouldn't be ready to move on to the next subject yet. That was Ollie, always needing to make sure the people he loved were okay.

"Is that really a question?" Miles countered. "This is me we're talking about."

The four men laughed. There was nothing in the world like laughing with them.

"I'm happy for you, Miles. And I like him," Ollie added.

Yeah…Miles liked him too. "So is this the only reason you guys came over? To bust my balls about Quinn, or what?"

"Is there a better reason than that?" Chance cocked a brow.

No, he guessed there wasn't. He damn sure would do the same if the situation were reversed.

The four friends continued to visit, outside of Wild Side, in a way they didn't do nearly enough of. Miles made coffee and they joked and laughed the way they always did together. Laughed in ways they couldn't do with anyone except each other.

They spoke more about Ollie's work helping at the LGBT

center with Austin, how Quinn could fit in, and about their recent discovery about Dare's past. It was amazing that you could know someone and not know important things about them. Not many people knew any of the important things that made Miles who he was—his situation that led him to his family and how it affected him to this day. He envied people like Quinn and Dare who could just move on or be open about their experiences, especially since they'd had it a whole lot harder than Miles had.

It was a couple hours later when they left. Miles closed the door with a smile on his face. Yes, he was growing up. Moving on. He was happy. And he couldn't help but wonder when he'd get to see Quinn again.

———⁓———

THE PAST FEW weeks had been crazy. Quinn and Miles were at each other's apartment every night. Miles's place was bigger, but Quinn had his computer equipment at home, so they ended up there pretty often. He wasn't sure he would ever be able to sleep alone again—not that it was a bad thing. He sure as hell liked sharing a bed with Miles every night, though he was still shocked it had happened. Surprised at where they'd found themselves. It was a far cry from a random hookup from a bar.

Quinn had never wanted to be with someone, wanted the same person the way he did with Miles.

They were kind of a big deal.

Chance, Oliver, and Matt never let Miles forget it, either.

The thought made him snicker. Quinn had joined them the past few Fridays at Wild Side and the crew was always teasing each other about something. Miles was the target most of the time, which was apparently different for them. Oliver said it used to be him, and Miles had been the worst about it, not that it surprised Quinn.

It did Miles some good to be on the receiving end of a little friendly razzing.

It was a Tuesday and Quinn was heading to the LGBT center to meet with Oliver and Austin. They'd set up the meeting to get some real planning done on the event they wanted to organize.

Quinn parked his car beside the large, white building with rainbow letters. As he got out, he heard, "Hey!" and realized he'd arrived at the same time as Oliver. He looked over and saw Oliver jogging toward him from a few rows away.

"Hey," Quinn replied when the other man reached him.

"Perfect timing." They headed for the door and signed in at the front desk. It was really incredible inside. There was a common room to the left with a TV, DVDs, billiards, air hockey and foosball tables.

"I can't believe I've never been here before." Quinn had driven past it a million times and never thought to come in, which was ridiculous. It should have been more important to him. He should have made time earlier to help.

"Yeah, I hear ya. I was the same way before I met Austin. I've really loved volunteering. It's a great program. They have a fantastic library, as well. It's cool to see so many youths have access to literature about people who share their stories and have been through what they're going through."

Yeah, yeah it was. Quinn had never even seen a place like this when he was younger. Not somewhere specifically queer related.

Oliver showed him the library, which was just as impressive as Oliver had said. Apparently, he was an author and had organized a book drive not too long ago. They'd acquired boxes upon boxes of LGBT books, according to Oliver.

"Come on," he told Quinn. "Austin's office is this way."

Oliver led him down a long hallway with rainbows and clouds painted along the walls. He stopped when he reached a door that was cracked open, and knocked. It was only a second later that Quinn heard Austin call for them to come in.

"Hey, good to see you both." He pushed his red hair off his forehead and then reached out for Quinn's hand, followed by Oliver's, shaking them both.

"Thanks for letting me join in with you guys. I'm really excited." He was incredibly excited. So excited that, "I'd really love to organize some kind of—well, I guess it would be like a field trip to my office. I think it would be really awesome if the kids were able to see our process and everything that goes into bringing a game from idea to an actuality."

Quinn pulled a piece of paper out of his pocket. "I checked prices on renting a bus. I'm not sure if we'd have that many youths who were interested, but I got the information anyway."

He set it on the desk in front of Austin, who smiled at him.

"I'm sure funds are tight around here but I bet we can work something out—fundraise or hell, I'd help and I know Miles would too." They'd already talked about it. "I'd love for them to see that you can do anything with your life, ya know? To show them anyone can have their dreams." He'd gone from a kid no one wanted to being happy, productive, and loved.

Oliver and Austin both watched him, making Quinn realize he'd taken over the conversation and rambled, hardly taking a breath between. Hell, he didn't even know what these men had planned. They were obviously more experienced with this than he was. "Sorry. I tend to get a little carried away when I'm excited about something. Just ask Miles." He winked and felt Oliver squeeze his shoulder as Austin chuckled.

"Excitement is good. I'm just a little blown away but in the best way. Some of the youth here mostly come for the social aspect and have loving families, but most are here because no one wanted them. Because they were disowned or knew they would be. So when people do want them, when they're passionate about helping? Well, it means everything to them, and to me." Austin nodded and a swell of pride filled Quinn's chest.

"I know what it's like not to be wanted," Quinn admitted and Austin frowned.

"I'm sorry. As you know, Dare does too."

It wasn't something anyone should have to deal with—especially not because of who they loved.

They were silent for a moment as though they all needed to compose themselves before they jumped back into planning.

They spent the next couple hours hammering out specifics. They decided on two events—the trip to Quinn's office and also a party at the center. Quinn would take care of getting televisions and games here, and Oliver was taking on the promotional aspect of the event and donations to help make it happen.

When he walked out of the center with Oliver—Miles's Oliver—at his side, he felt a sense of satisfaction he wasn't sure he'd ever experienced. It had been years since he'd felt like he lacked anything in his life. He'd made his own way, had a career he loved, friends, happiness, but now? Helping here and having Miles, he realized that maybe he hadn't been as together as he'd thought. Maybe he hadn't always been as happy as he'd thought either.

As though Oliver read his mind, he said, "You make him happy. I've never seen him like this."

Quinn shrugged. "He does the same for me. He's…special."

"He is, though I don't really think he ever realized it."

No, he hadn't. He played it off well but Miles had always struggled inside. "I know," Quinn replied. "I don't think he feels like he has a right to mourn people he never knew, and I think he also might feel like it's a betrayal to his parents. He's more honorable than he wants people to know."

Oliver stilled. His brows pulled together. "He told you about being abandoned?" There was an incredible sense of shock in Oliver's voice.

"Yeah."

"Wow... Miles doesn't do that."

"He did it for me," Quinn admitted. He didn't want to come off as an asshole but he was proud of being important to Miles, because Miles sure as fuck was important to him.

Oliver sighed and leaned against Quinn's car. "It's always been hard on him. He doesn't get close to anyone because he doesn't trust. He's afraid of being left behind or somehow being betrayed, so if he keeps the people who matter to him to a minimum, he lessens the chance of that happening. There's always a push and pull with Miles. He holds on to me and Chance so damn tightly, that it could feel stifling at times. Not that we don't love him, because we do."

There wasn't a part of Quinn that doubted that. He could see where Oliver was coming from. Could see how Miles would do that.

"It was just hard at times. It felt like bringing anyone else in was a betrayal to Miles, when we would never walk away from him. We've always loved him and as much as he knows that, fear is a powerful emotion. He struggled with Matt a lot in the beginning."

"Yeah, he told me that too," Quinn admitted. And Oliver was right. People often underestimated the power of fear. If they didn't experience it themselves, they couldn't understand it. It wasn't logical, or why couldn't you get over it? Unfortunately, life wasn't always that easy. It wasn't always black and white.

Oliver added, "He's always played a sort of tug-o-war with himself. He loves his parents. He's damn proud to be a

Sorenson, but I think the not knowing is a constant struggle for him. The not knowing why, or who they are. Loyalty and honesty are two of the most important things to Miles."

"It's hard to close the door on something if you don't know what it is. Curiosity is a motherfucker," Quinn said. "I asked him if he'd ever looked for his parents—just to see what he could find, but he shot me down."

"That doesn't surprise me at all," Oliver replied. "Anyway, I just wanted to make sure you understood him a bit and also that you know how good you are for him. I never expected this for Miles. Matt, Chance, and I love him and we're grateful he found you."

Goddamn, Quinn's pulse sped up. This conversation meant more to him than he could put into words. "Thank you. I'm glad I found him too." And then because he really thought he needed to lighten the mood, he added, "It's this ass. Brings down the strongest of men."

Oliver laughed, and they said their goodbyes not long afterward. As he sat in his car, his phone vibrated telling him he had a text message.

Counselor: How'd it go? Miles asked him. He'd changed the name in his phone a week before.

Perfect, Quinn replied. Everything was perfect.

CHAPTER TWENTY-THREE

"**H**ONEY! I'M HOME!" Quinn called out as he entered Miles's apartment.

Fuck. He closed his eyes just as his mom asked, "Who was that?" She'd called him a little while ago, and he'd hoped to be able to finish up the call before Quinn arrived. Obviously, that didn't happen.

"Was that Chance? Or Oliver?" she asked again. "Those boys are so silly."

He could end this right now. He could pretend it was one of his friends, and she would never know the difference, but when he opened his mouth, that's not what came out. "No, it's not Chance or Oliver, Mom."

"Matt then? How's his music coming along?"

Quinn covered his mouth, his eyes apologizing for bursting in the way he did. It was that action that made Miles need to be honest with her even more. Quinn shouldn't feel bad about this. They were in a relationship. He had nothing to hide.

"No, it's not Matty either… It's the man I'm seeing. His name is Quinn."

Quinn stopped dead in his tracks.

His mom gasped, and damn it. Now Quinn was making a

heart out of his hands. He pointed to Miles, then made another heart, and pointed to himself. *You love me.* Fucker. He couldn't even say *I love you* it had to be *you love me.*

Miles flipped him off.

"Who are you and what did you do with my son?" his mom finally asked.

"What's with people and saying that? Chance thought I'd been abducted by aliens. He even searched the pantry for me, though I'm not sure why that's where he thought I'd be."

"Well, you have to admit…it's different. But good, too. Oh! Are you bringing him to dinner tomorrow night?"

Well, shit. He hadn't even thought about that. He hadn't planned on telling his parents about Quinn just yet, but then opportunity knocked. "I don't know. We'll see. He might have other plans tomorrow night." He went from admitting he was dating someone, to his parents wanting to meet them. This was like the Wild Side meeting on crack.

"I really hope he can make it. Your father will be home. I can't wait to tell him."

Miles rolled his eyes. He was so fucked. "Okay, Mom. I'm going to go. I'll see you tomorrow, okay?"

He could practically hear her smile through the phone. "I love you. Oh my God, I'm so happy! I can't believe you finally have a boyfriend! I was jealous of Viv ever since Ollie settled down."

Only his mother would be so excited about this. "I love you too," he told her and hung up before she had the chance to say anything else.

"I don't," Quinn said the second Miles was off the phone.

"You don't what?"

"Have plans tomorrow night. I also love dinner. I've never had dinner with parents but I think I would love that too."

Miles's stomach flipped and a smile tugged at his lips. Goddamn, he was wrapped up in this man. He walked over to Quinn and fingered a strand of his hair. "Do you want to go to dinner at my parents' house tomorrow night?"

"Nah, I'm good," Quinn replied, and Miles grabbed his chin.

"So fucking naughty. Am I going to have to teach you a lesson?"

"I hope so."

"Be careful what you wish for." Miles cocked a brow at him. "If you're not good, I'll tie you up and throw you over my shoulder and drag you there." He wanted Quinn to go, he realized it then. He really fucking wanted it.

"The way to a man's dick is through ropes. At least mine." Quinn winked and Miles kissed him. He pushed his tongue past Quinn's lips and pulled his hair, then thought about shoving him to his knees before realizing he wanted Quinn's dick in his mouth instead.

He dropped down and blew him and after swallowing his load, Miles stood and kissed him again. "Go to dinner at my parents' house tomorrow night." This time, it wasn't a question.

Quinn winked. "Yes, sir," he said as he tucked his dick back into his pants. He didn't bother buttoning or zipping them. "Oh, and today. It was fucking incredible, Miles. I wish you could have been there. Austin is really excited about all the ideas I pitched to him. Ollie is on board to help—I fucking love him, by the way. We talked about you and how I won you over with my sparkling personality."

"Personality? Oh no, baby boy. It was your ass that won me over."

"Okay, well that's actually what I told him."

Miles sat at the bar while Quinn grabbed a package of microwave popcorn from the pantry. It was strange seeing someone so at home in his place. It was as though Quinn had been walking around his kitchen forever. As though it belonged to him as well. Somehow, it was…comforting.

"So you guys got it all worked out?" he asked.

"Yeah. I like Austin. And like I said, Oliver, of course. He loves you a great deal."

Yeah, Miles knew he did. He knew Chance and Matt did as well. He was so fucking lucky. Why couldn't he always concentrate on that instead of worry about other shit?

"It's interesting…hearing you talk about my friends this way. I like having you in that part of my life."

"I like being there." Quinn put the bag in the microwave and turned it on. When it was done, they moved to the couch and Quinn finished telling him about his meeting with Austin and Oliver.

"He said Matt was at school," Quinn told him before tossing a piece of popcorn into his mouth. "I was thinking about something but I wanted to run it by you first."

Miles nodded, feeling a twinge of unexplained nerves in his gut. "Yeah?"

"I can't make any promises. I want to say that up front, but I remember Matt talking about his music last week and…Jesus, it means a lot to him. I know that feeling and I just…I was thinking, I wonder if he's ever considered trying to write music for video games? It might not be his end game, but hell, maybe it's something that could help him along the way. It would give him a chance to do what he loves, and in case you didn't know, I have a bit of an *in* where video games are concerned."

Quinn shrugged. "Again, I can't make promises but I'd help out as much as I could. I didn't want to bring it up to Matt or Oliver before talking to you first—to see if you thought it was a good idea, or hell, because I already feel like I'm encroaching on your life as it is but—"

"Stop." Miles reached out and put a finger to Quinn's lips. Quinn wanting to help his friend like that? It meant the world to Miles. "You got me turned inside out, Quinn. Like I don't know up from down. Like I don't know myself."

Quinn frowned. "This is a good thing, right?"

Yes. It was a very good thing. "Thank you. It means a lot to me that you want to help Matt. You don't have to ask my permission for stuff like this either. They…they're your friends now, too."

And that didn't hurt nearly as much as he thought it would. He wasn't going to lose them. Because they loved him and Quinn did too.

"I FEEL LIKE I'm getting sent to the principal's office."

Miles glanced over at Quinn in the passenger seat. "What? How does that make sense? Because you're going to meet my parents?"

It made sense inside his head. "I don't know. Maybe that's not a good comparison but...I don't know. I feel like they're going to be leery of me. You just told them about me, and now I'm going home with you? And what if they don't like me?" He'd never worried about someone liking him in his life. Quinn was who he was, and that wouldn't change, but then he'd never met the parents of someone he was in love with before, either.

"Wow...you're really worried about this. How cute."

Quinn turned to him. "How cute? You're a dickhead. Here I'm worried as hell about what your parents will think of me and you say it's cute."

"That's because you're cute."

"I hate you."

"They'll love you."

Quinn perked up at that. "They will love me, won't they?"

Miles laughed and some of the tension in the car melted away with it. This was new territory for both of them. Quinn knew Miles was nervous, as well. He'd never taken someone home, and Quinn had never gone home with someone.

Hell, he'd forgotten what home and family were even like.

They were quiet the rest of the drive to Beverly Hills. When they pulled up in front of a large, white home with a circular driveway and pillars, Quinn asked, "Do we still have time to change our minds?"

"If we make a break for it now, they'll never know. I can fake sick again and spend the evening fucking you instead."

That sounded like a good idea to Quinn.

When the door opened, and a woman with long, blond hair stepped out, he knew they were fucked.

"Damn it. A few seconds too late," Miles said before reaching over and squeezing Quinn's leg. "It'll be okay."

Then, as though he just realized what he said, he added, "Holy shit. Maybe Chance was right. Maybe I *was* kidnapped by aliens...."

They laughed together, and goddamn it felt good to laugh with Miles.

"I'm going to have to be real nasty to you tonight to make up for being all soft now."

Quinn cocked a brow at him. "I'm looking forward do it."

"Let's go before she comes after us."

They got out of the car, and Quinn waited for Miles to walk around the vehicle before they made their way to the porch. His mom went straight for Quinn first. He held out his hand, but she ignored it and pulled him into a hug. "I'm Veronica. It's so nice to meet you."

Quinn immediately hugged her back. He liked her already because this one action showed how much she loved her son. "I'm Quinn. It's great to meet you as well."

"I see where I rank," Miles said playfully as his mother pulled away.

"Oh stop." She swatted his arm. "You know I love you."

They hugged, and then Veronica led them in the house. The second the door closed, Quinn heard another one open. "Damn it! I'm late but only by a couple minutes!" a man's voice said.

He came down the hallway, with salt and pepper hair and a kind smile and wearing a suit.

"I made him promise to be out of his office before you both arrived," Veronica told them.

"Two minutes! I was only two minutes late!" he replied.

"That's not late, Mom. That's early," Miles added and his father's eyes glowed.

"See? Miles always understands me."

"Oh, so he got *workaholic* from you?" Quinn asked.

Miles growled and Veronica laughed.

"I have no idea what you're talking about," Miles's father said before holding out his hand. "Tyson Sorenson, nice to meet you."

Well, that was proper as fuck. "Quinn, and right back at ya."

"Do you guys want a drink?" Veronica asked.

They all nodded and then made their way into the large kitchen. It looked like a spot where they congregated often. There was a window seat and a bar; some paperwork was on the counter that told Quinn Tyson had done some work there as well.

"What would you like to drink, Quinn?" Veronica asked.

Before Quinn could reply, Miles answered, "I got it, Mom."

"You didn't ask the man what he wants?"

Miles winked at her. "I know what the man wants."

Oh, Jesus Christ. Who the fuck was this guy and what did he do with Miles? He went to the fridge and grabbed two bottles of beer. Miles opened the first and handed it to Quinn.

"Thanks."

Before opening his own, he plucked a bottle of wine from the rack and opened that as well. He filled two glasses and handed those to his parents.

"Oh, Miles. I wanted to ask you about the Johnson case. He—"

"Lied to me, the little shit," Miles replied. "I had to rework his—"

"There's no work at family dinner!" Veronica interrupted them. "Not while Quinn is here." She glanced at him and mouthed, "Thank you," making Quinn laugh.

"But Vero...just one thing?" Tyson asked.

It was incredible watching them. Their personalities were so different from Miles. He could see the love between the three of them. Could see that Miles knew he could let his guard down there and that he did.

"Fine. We'll just cook dinner then." Tyson winked at Veronica, who smiled. It made Quinn lock eyes with Miles, who gave him a quick nod.

He knew it meant the world for Quinn to be here. To be around Miles's family.

"Wash your hands, Quinn. We all help around here."

Quinn's heart sped up and damned if it didn't feel like the damn thing was growing. "I'm on it, Counselor."

CHAPTER TWENTY-FOUR

Q UINN FIT IN well with his family.

If Miles were being honest, he'd admit that Quinn probably fit in better than he did. Quinn and Miles's father made joke after joke all evening. At one point, he was pretty sure they were in a competition—both wanting to be the one to make everyone else laugh the most.

Quinn asked his mom about her charity work and told her what he had planned with Oliver and Austin.

She cried, because that's what his mom did, but he knew then and there his mom had fallen in love with Quinn.

They'd made eggplant parmesan together and ate sitting around the table. Miles was quiet most of the time—letting Quinn and his parents control the conversation. He'd much rather sit back and watch. Examine. He enjoyed seeing Quinn interact with his family, enjoyed the way he fell right into place with them in a way Miles struggled to do with outsiders.

When they finished dinner, they continued to sit at the table—Quinn and Miles enjoying another beer and his parents drinking their wine.

"Do you have any family in the area?" his mom asked Quinn. Miles froze up but Quinn didn't. He took it in stride the way he did with everything.

"No. I never knew my father. I lost my mother when I was young, and since we didn't have any other family, I grew up in the system."

"Oh, I'm sorry. I didn't realize," she replied. Miles draped his arm around the back of Quinn's chair and squeezed his neck in support.

"It's fine. You couldn't have known. I've made peace with my past. Things weren't great, but they could have been worse. I have a lot of respect for people who foster children. There are a lot of great ones out there, unfortunately, I wasn't the ideal child."

Miles frowned. Quinn was right. Yes, there were wonderful people out there who took in children, but he also wouldn't let Quinn take all the blame. "And there are not so good situations too, where children have to survive things no one should."

Quinn glanced at him appreciatively and winked.

His parents were both quiet, and he knew they were taking in what they heard. That they respected the hell out of Quinn for being so open and honest and strong.

Miles himself wasn't that strong. He hadn't suffered nearly what Quinn had yet he had built walls around himself Quinn never had.

"Do we want to set a weekend for our annual Big Bear trip?" his mom asked, obviously trying to change the subject.

"We have a cabin by Big Bear Lake. Mom drags Dad and me up once a year, and we're not allowed to work," Miles explained to Quinn.

"Kind of like our beach trip when you called off?" Quinn asked.

"I knew it!" his mom replied. "I knew you weren't sick. Thank you, Quinn."

"No problem," he replied to her.

Miles and his father pulled out their phones and began going over their schedules. They decided on a weekend a month from then.

"You're welcome to go, Quinn. We'd love it if you could make it," his mom said, and Quinn's eyes darted up before he looked over at Miles. He wanted to go, wanted to go so fucking badly. Miles could see it in his expression and the set of his shoulders, but he wasn't sure how Miles would take it.

"You should go." Miles shrugged but then felt like a dick. "I'd like for you to go."

"I'll check my schedule," Quinn said teasingly. Miles rolled his eyes, and his parents laughed.

They spoke for a few more minutes before Miles heard, "Can I borrow Miles for just a few minutes? We'll do dishes at the same time," from his dad. They couldn't be around each other without talking work.

"Go ahead," Quinn told him while his mom said, "Sold!"

She said that because she wanted a moment alone with Quinn, and Miles knew it. Otherwise, she would have fought the work talk.

She pushed to her feet. "Grab your drink, Quinn, and let's get the hell out of here!"

They scrambled out of the kitchen, without a backward glance. The second they were gone, his dad said, "You're in love with him."

"Yeah," Miles admitted. "Yeah, I am."

QUINN SAT IN the living room with Veronica. He could see the questions exploding in her eyes. She wanted to know about him and Miles. Wanted to know how serious they were.

"No one else would have been able to get Miles to call off work," she told him.

"I know," Quinn answered, because he did. "I love him. I know you needed to hear that and I do. I won't hurt him."

Immediately, her body relaxed. She obviously loved her son very much. "I'm sorry. I know it's not my business and I'm not typically forcing myself into Miles's private life like that, but this is very different for him—bringing you home and introducing you to Chance, Oliver, and Matt. Even the calling off work. He doesn't do things like that. He never has. I love him with all my heart. I just have to make sure he's okay."

Quinn nodded, feeling a tightness in his chest. He wished he could have this conversation with his own mom. She would have loved Miles. He knew it. She would have supported anything Quinn did in his life.

"He told me...I know the circumstances around his adoption—his abandonment."

She lifted a shaky hand to her mouth. "He was so little. You'd never know it seeing him now, but he was...so little and fragile. I took one look at him and knew he was supposed to be mine. It's hard for him. He loves us. There is not a doubt in my mind about that, but he's so damn proud. So hard on himself. He's so afraid to put his heart out there, because if he holds it close, he won't get hurt. He hasn't come to peace with it."

No, no he hadn't. That was the difference between them, but in Quinn's case, his mother—the person who was supposed to love him the most in the world—hadn't chosen to leave him. She hadn't wrapped him in a blanket and thrown him away. She'd been forced to leave him.

For Miles, there were questions, so many fucking questions, that Quinn had no doubt slowly ate away at him.

Miles was an answers person. He'd told Quinn that, but the biggest, most defining moment in his life, he had no answers for.

For someone who so badly needed *one plus one to make two*, that had to be brutal. Quinn had no doubt that was why he struggled to get past it.

"I won't hurt him," Quinn said again, because it was all he could say.

"Yes," she smiled at him. "I know you won't. And you're welcome here with Miles any time, okay? I kind of like you." She winked and yeah, he really liked her too.

There was a noise behind him, and Quinn turned around to see Miles and his father step into the room.

"Are you done talking about me yet?" Miles asked.

Quinn stood up. "Perfect timing. We just finished."

CHAPTER TWENTY-FIVE

"**D**O YOU MIND if we go to my place?" Miles asked when they got to the car.

"Sure. No problem," Quinn replied. He never minded being at Miles's place. He just wished he had his equipment there. "I like your parents." Quinn glanced at Miles in the darkened car, as he pulled onto the road.

"They're incredible," Miles answered softly. Quinn reached over and set his hand on Miles's thigh. They drove the rest of the way home like that, Quinn touching him. Every once in a while, Miles would set his hand on top of Quinn's, or hold it, until he needed it on the steering wheel again.

When they got inside Miles's apartment, which was lit up by the lights of the city shining through the oversized windows, Miles stopped, grabbed Quinn's face in two hands and said, "Thank you."

"I should be the one thanking you. You gave me a night with family." Which was exactly how it had felt to Quinn. Maybe it wasn't his family, but for a few hours, it felt like it.

"You're always welcome. They'll love you just like a son."

Those words filled Quinn's chest. Forced the blood through his veins, giving him life. Miles gave him life.

"Can I play with you tonight?" Miles's voice was rough, raw, like sandpaper against his skin when he was craving something coarse.

"Is that really a question?" He'd play any time Miles wanted-ed.

Miles ran his hands down Quinn's back. "Can I tie you up?"

He grinned. "I'd be disappointed if you didn't."

"Oh fuck. You're killing me, baby boy. Already got me all tied up." Miles buried his face in Quinn's neck, before biting it and then licking the sting away.

"You got me tied up, too."

Miles growled and lifted him. He carried Quinn to his bed. The moon was bright and high in the sky. That coupled with the city lights illuminated the room well.

Miles set him on his feet next to the bed. "Take your clothes off," he told Quinn before turning and walking to his closet. Quinn stripped quickly. When Miles stepped out of the closet with a box, Quinn was standing there nude, waiting to be told what to do next.

Miles walked over to him and set the box on the bed. He twined his fingers through Quinn's hair and said, "Jesus, you are so goddamned beautiful."

"You're not so bad yourself," Quinn replied, using the same line on Miles that Miles had used on him before. He winked and in return received a smile from Miles.

"Now, take my clothes off."

Quinn slid Miles's shirt up his torso. Miles lifted his arms and Quinn pulled it off. He rubbed his thumbs over Miles's nipples. Leaned forward and kissed his collarbone. Tasted sweat on his skin.

"You're getting sidetracked," Miles said when Quinn lashed him with his tongue.

"You taste good." He ran his tongue down the side of Miles's neck.

"Pants."

"You never let me play," Quinn replied, before getting to work on Miles's jeans. He unbuttoned and unzipped them, kneeled and took his pants off. When he got to Miles's shoes, he pulled off one, then the other before finishing with his jeans and underwear.

Talk about gorgeous. He was so damn muscular—tight, dark skin stretched across perfect bones and firm muscles.

Quinn cupped his heavy balls. Wanted to lap at them, to suck Miles till he could drink down his load, but he didn't; instead, he again waited for Miles to tell him what to do next.

He loved this, waiting and wanting while his lover tortured him. It wasn't always like this. Yes, Miles was always more dominant when they fucked than Quinn was, but they didn't consistently *play*. Tonight, they both wanted to play.

"Go ahead. You can lick it. Only for a moment, though."

So Quinn did. He licked the head of Miles's fat cock. Ran his tongue down the length. Laved Miles's nuts and rubbed his cheek against Miles's pubic hair, before Miles told him, "That's enough. I'll lose it if you keep going and I want to savor you."

He pulled Quinn to his feet and kissed him hard and deep.

Let his tongue probe Quinn's mouth, tangle with his own. He tasted like beer and Miles. Smelled like strength and man.

"Lie down," Miles told him, and Quinn did. Miles moved over and straddled him before opening the box and pulling out a piece of soft, red rope. "Wrists."

Quinn held them out, excitement singing down his spine. He wanted this, wanted to be bound and at Miles's mercy. Wanted it so fucking badly with this man he loved.

He placed a cloth around Quinn's wrists, concentrated hard as he wrapped the rope over it. He obviously knew what he was doing when it came to knots because he twined it just right, so Quinn's wrists were tied together, with a loop at the top. Quinn wondered what Miles's plans were for that knot.

"Well, aren't you fancy?" he teased.

"Fucker." Miles grinned.

"I didn't know you could do this."

"I can." He climbed off Quinn and sat beside him. "I want your ass nice and red for me first. Roll over."

Quinn went willingly. Fucking eagerly.

"Hands above your head," Miles instructed. When Quinn complied, Miles hooked the loop on the rope over the middle section of his headboard. It was the least modern thing in his apartment, the two curved lines on either side of the head-board, with a spindle-shaped knob in the center that stood taller. It was perfect for keeping Quinn's hands in place.

"Huh. I just thought that was for decoration."

"It is, but I kept imagining you there, so I thought we'd try it."

Translation: Miles had never tied anyone else to this spot on his bed. That made Quinn feel…a smile spread across his face as he looked over his shoulder at Miles.

"Oh, proud of yourself, are you?"

"Maybe a little…" Quinn joked.

"Such a cocky boy."

"Then teach me a lesson," Quinn encouraged.

"Oh, I plan to. Paddle, hand, or crop?" Miles asked and Quinn trembled, fucking trembled, and bucked his hips against the bed, eager for the pleasure Miles would give him.

"Paddle," Quinn answered.

"That would have been my choice too."

Over his shoulder, Quinn watched as Miles pulled a small paddle out of the box. He rubbed a hand over Quinn's ass first, making him shudder again.

"My God, this ass," Miles said before his hand came down on Quinn's cheeks a couple times, warming him up. Each time hand met skin, heat rushed through him. Went straight to his dick and balls. His cock ached. His balls were plump and full and…*smack!* Quinn shuddered. Goddamn that burn was his favorite thing in the world.

It wasn't long before Miles picked up the paddle. He leaned forward and kissed Quinn's left ass cheek, then his right, before he pulled back and it was then the paddle kissing Quinn's ass.

"Fuck." His eyes rolled back in his head when the wood met his flesh. He ground his molars together and arched his ass out toward Miles, needing more.

Skin-to-skin, Miles's hand was on his ass again, rubbing gently. "I got you, baby boy. I'll give you what you need."

His words made Quinn relax his hips, lie flat on the bed and wait for Miles to do him right, the way Quinn knew he would.

Smack. The paddle came down on him again and again. His ass scalded with a delicious fucking heat. A prickling feeling started at the base of his spine, spread out into a hot tingling sensation that was powerful enough to make Quinn lose his damn mind.

A bead of sweat rolled down his forehead before the paddle was gone. Miles lay on top of him, the pressure against him making his flaming ass feel even better.

"How did I find you?" Miles asked, close to his ear before licking a bead of sweat from Quinn's temple. "You are… God, you're *everything*, and I'd be lying if I didn't admit that still scares the fuck out of me." He wrapped his arms around Quinn, rubbed his cock up and down Quinn's crack. "I don't want it to. I don't want to fear you, but I do. I've never been scared of another person in my life."

Quinn's heart banged against his chest, beat Miles's name.

Quinn tried to lower his arms, but the tug of the ropes stopped him. He'd forgotten he was tied up.

"I won't hurt you. I won't leave you. Couldn't even if I wanted to. You do me too good." There was more to it than that, of course, but he knew those words were exactly what Miles needed to hear.

He growled in Quinn's ear, kissed his way down Quinn's

back. Licked Quinn's stinging ass cheeks, then bit, making Quinn arch off the bed.

"Really gonna need you inside me soon. You know how much my hole likes you." He wiggled his ass against Miles's groin.

Miles leaned up, spread Quinn's cheeks, and spit before rubbing his cock up and down Quinn's crack, teasing him. "You know how much my dick likes your hole."

Quinn chuckled. "Has it ever been like this for you before? The laughing…the playfulness?"

Miles stopped moving, went silent for a moment. "No. Never. Only you."

It was Quinn's turn to growl when Miles lifted off of him. He didn't go far, just released the rope from the knob and flipped Quinn over. "That going to be okay on your ass?" he asked.

"That's going to be perfect on my ass."

"Good. I'll rub cream on it later. Keep your arms down for a moment. Don't want you to get hurt."

Before Quinn could reply, Miles leaned over him, sucked Quinn's cock deep into his mouth. Nuzzled his face in Quinn's balls, while Quinn kept his arms down to get the blood flowing through them again.

"Fuck, that feels so good. We're in dangerous territory here."

Miles looked up at him and smiled. "Such an easy trigger. You can't come too soon, so that means it's my turn."

Miles climbed over him, straddled Quinn's chest, Quinn's

arms beneath him. He kneeled, angled his dick toward Quinn's mouth and Quinn opened hungrily for him. He wanted to drink him down, take him as far back as he could, suck Miles's dick like his life depended on it.

Miles pushed in, groaned as Quinn swallowed around his cock.

"Love that you can almost take all of me."

Quinn wanted to tell Miles it was because he was so fucking good, but it was kind of hard to talk with a mouth full of dick.

He sucked Miles as best he could, let his lover thrust in his mouth, and just when he thought Miles was going to lose it, when he thought Miles would be the one coming too soon, he jerked back.

He moved off Quinn, rubbed his arms. "Will they be okay if I hook you back up?" he asked, so much damn care in his voice.

"Yes."

Quinn raised his arms over his head, and Miles latched the loop in the rope again. Afterward, he dug around in the nightstand and grabbed lube and a condom.

Once he was suited up, Miles dripped lube on his prick and rubbed it as he climbed between Quinn's legs.

He squirted more lube on his fingers. Quinn lifted his legs close to his chest, and damned if his eyes didn't flutter when Miles rubbed his hole.

"I love how hungry your ass is for me—how much you love your hole played with."

Quinn grinned loopily. He felt like he was high, bouncing on clouds or some shit. "It's my most favorite thing."

That earned him another laugh from Miles, but then as he angled his cock toward Quinn's ring—as he slowly pushed in, their eyes locked together in what felt like an unbreakable hold—everything got real fucking serious, real fucking quick.

"Oh God. I could live inside of you," Miles said as he pushed in balls deep. He held Quinn's legs open and against his chest, without taking his eyes off Quinn's, and started to fuck. No, started to make love to him.

He pushed in real slow, real deep before pulling out. He rolled his hips and each time he slammed in, he hit Quinn's prostate just right.

They were two bodies working together in unison, two bodies that somehow felt as one.

"I don't know what I want to watch more—your eyes or the way my dick stretches your hole. The way you open up for me, grip me real fucking good." Miles's eyes darted down, between them. "It's fucking beautiful, baby boy. Your ass taking me."

"Oh God, yes." Quinn's eyes fluttered again. His dick leaked all over his stomach. His balls were so damn full. And when Miles leaned over, when he parted Quinn's mouth with his tongue before pushing it in deep, Quinn was done for.

Miles wrapped a hand around his dick and stroked twice, a long rope of come shooting between them. He bucked his hips, stroked again and shot for a second time as he saw stars behind his eyes.

Miles cursed, fucked harder, deeper, called out Quinn's name, then crashed their mouths together again as he came. He didn't rest on top of Quinn long, though. He ran his hand between them, in Quinn's load, and sucked it from his fingers before removing the rope and untying Quinn's wrists.

He ripped the condom off, tossed it, and lay on top of Quinn, kissing his neck, licking his ear.

When they came down from their high, Miles rolled over, tucking Quinn in the crook of his arm.

"Can I tell you something?" Miles asked.

"Is it how good I work your dick?" Quinn joked, but Miles didn't take the bait and he realized this was serious. "Yeah, of course. You can tell me anything."

"I've thought about it...trying to find them. Just to know."

Quinn closed his eyes, let Miles's words and pain wash over him. Wished he could take it away.

"I lied to you," Miles continued. "Our first weekend together when I said there was nothing I had the balls to do? Searching for them. I don't have the guts to do it. And when I used to walk down by the homeless? I was looking for them. Thought that I would see myself in someone's eyes, but I never did."

"Oh, Miles." Quinn leaned closer, kissed his guy's neck. Nuzzled him. "I love you."

"I know. I love you too." Miles sighed. "Maybe I could make peace with it if I knew...but then I remember, what is there to make peace with? One or both of them left me. They left me to die. What more do I need to know than that?"

Quinn's heart broke at the pain in Miles's voice. This time, he pushed up on his elbow, looked down at Miles's whiskey-colored eyes. "There are a million different possibilities. Maybe they were sick. On drugs. Have gotten help. Maybe your mom did it and your dad didn't know or your dad did it and your mom didn't know. That doesn't excuse it. Jesus, it doesn't, but it kills me for you to not feel wanted. You are so fucking loved, Miles. Your mom and dad, who I met tonight. Chance, Oliver, Matt…me. Whatever reason your parents, or hell, whoever the fuck it was, who did what they did—whatever the reason, it doesn't change how much we love you. Nothing will."

"I know." Miles gave Quinn a sad smile. He didn't believe him. Quinn could see that.

"I'm serious."

"I know you are, baby boy. I get it. I know I'm lucky. Everyone wasn't as lucky as I am."

He meant Quinn but Quinn shook that off. "I have everything I need."

"Yeah," Miles replied. "I do too." But it still didn't sound like he believed it.

CHAPTER TWENTY-SIX

T HE PAST COUPLE weeks had been incredible.

Miles and Quinn spent nearly all their spare time together—Fridays at Wild Side, dinner after work, nights in one another's beds.

If Miles hadn't realized he'd been addicted to Quinn before, he definitely knew he was now.

The night they had dinner with his parents solidified things between them. Quinn was a major part of his life, which was exactly where Miles wanted him.

He sure as shit wished he wasn't sitting in his office right now with another three hours left of work to go. It was Friday night, and he wanted to pick up his guy and go spend the evening at Wild Side with their friends.

Not just Miles's friends. *Their* friends.

He leaned back in his chair just as his cell buzzed. Miles plucked it off the desk to see a text from the object of his fascination.

You picking me up for Wild Side tonight, Counselor, or do you want me to meet you at your apartment? I'm home early today.

It was never a question of whether Quinn would or wouldn't go. He belonged there.

I'll come to your place. Be naked and I'll do a few really dirty things to you before we go.

Quinn replied back, **Counting on it.**

Miles chuckled just as there was a soft knock on his office door, before it pushed open. His father stuck his head in. "What are you smiling about?" he asked as he made his way inside the office.

"Nothing," Miles answered automatically but then added, "Quinn." He was like a lovesick puppy—ridiculously cheesy and doe-eyed over his boyfriend.

"It's good to see you like this. Your mother and I are over the moon." His dad sat in the chair on the opposite side of Miles's cherry-wood desk.

"I am too," Miles admitted. It felt good to be happy. To trust someone enough to let them in.

"You really are in love with him, aren't you?"

Miles thought about the way Quinn made him feel, the way he made Miles laugh and open up and live his life. Thought about the kind of man Quinn was and the things he'd been through and the honesty he'd shared with Miles. "Yes, I am. I'm actually finding it hard to concentrate on work, if you can believe that."

"Holy shit. Now I'm worried!" His dad winked, and both men laughed. He loved the man sitting in front of him. He and Miles's mom had chosen him, had taken him home and loved him with their whole hearts every day of his life.

That was all that mattered. That should be all that mattered.

"I've never thanked you," Miles said softly.

"Thanked me for what?"

He answered honestly, simply, "For being my father."

"You don't have to thank me for that. Raising you has been the single biggest joy in mine and your mother's lives. We wouldn't be complete without you. You've been my best friend, son, and now my work confidant. I should be thanking you."

Miles shook that off. The idea of it was absurd, but he appreciated the sentiment. "I guess it was just meant to be, wasn't it?" he asked, to which his father nodded.

"What brought this on all of a sudden?"

He shrugged. "I don't know." And he didn't. Miles glanced at his phone and groaned. "Has it only been ten minutes? I think this is the longest day in history."

"I guess it's a good thing you're one of the bosses then." His dad pushed to his feet. "You want out of here early, then leave. Go have fun. Surprise Quinn. Maybe I'll do that with your mother too."

Miles tried to speak but damn near choked on his own words he was so shocked. He coughed, pounded on his chest and said, "Are you serious?"

"Why not? We work our asses off all the time. Your happiness is inspiring me to take a little extra time with your mom. You only live once, right?"

Yes, yes you did. His father was right and Miles not only loved the idea of getting out of there early and surprising Quinn, but he knew his mother would be thrilled if his dad did the same thing.

"Let's do it."

Miles pushed to his feet, and he and his father did just that.

⁓⁓⁓

AFTER PARKING AT Quinn's building, Miles shot him a quick text. **I don't want to do my work today and it's all your fault.**

He didn't have to wait long for a reply. **Oh, poor baby. That must suck. I just jacked off and now I'm getting in the shower.** A picture came through with the text of a smiling Quinn standing in his bathroom.

The bastard was trying to rub it in but what he didn't realize was this would be perfect for Miles. **I hate you**, he replied.

I love you! Quinn shot back, and Miles got out of the car, with the plan of using the key Quinn had given him for the first time.

Miles made his way through the building and took the elevator up. When he got to Quinn's door, he paused for a moment, reconsidering bursting in when Quinn didn't expect him.

But it would surprise him... Quinn was forever keeping Miles on his toes and for once, Miles wanted to be the one to do that to Quinn.

His heart skittered with excitement as he opened the door. The living room was empty the way he hoped it would be. He heard the water running down the hall, which confirmed Quinn was just where he said he would be.

Miles stripped his suit jacket off as he made his way down

the hallway. His fingers were shaking he was so fucking thrilled. He just began working his tie loose when his eyes snagged on a printout beside Quinn's computer.

It was as though he took a blow to the head. His vision went blurry. His head spun. His heart pounded in his ears and he thought for sure he would have a heart attack.

He rubbed the heels of his hands against his eyes. Stumbled on weak legs closer to the desk, picked up the paper and saw eyes he'd seen every day of his life. Eyes he saw every time he looked in the mirror, only the picture wasn't him.

His birth mom. There was no question in his mind that he was looking at a picture of his birth mom.

Miles rifled through the notebook on the desk. Saw Sacramento circled. Was he from Sacramento? If so, how did he get to Los Angeles? Thea Jane Clements. His mom's name? Was that his mother's name?

The paper became an extension of his hand and trembled.

Quinn had done this. Quinn had gone behind his back and looked for his family without his permission. He'd dug into Miles's family, into his life without Miles's permission. He'd betrayed not only Miles, but his parents too—the people who'd raised him and loved him and the man who just talked Miles into leaving work early to come and see Quinn.

My mom…this is my mom…

The mother who hadn't wanted him. The person who'd swaddled him in a blanket and threw him away.

Miles crumpled the papers in his fist. Squeezed his eyes closed so he didn't lash out and punch something. His head pounded. He gasped for breath and a sharp pain shot through his chest.

He couldn't remember making the decision to go to Quinn's room, couldn't remember how he got there. He only knew that one moment he was in the living room and the next he stepped into Quinn's bathroom just as Quinn stepped out of the shower. "What the fuck is this?" He threw the balled-up paper at Quinn.

Miles could see the realization on Quinn's face, in his eyes, the moment he realized what Miles had seen.

"It was not your place! You had no fucking right to do that, Quinn. None."

"Let me explain—"

"Fuck your explanation! You had no goddamn right. This, my life, is none of your fucking business. You don't get to make these decisions for me. You don't get to make this call, and fuck you for trying to. I trusted you." Miles fisted his hands. Closed his eyes and wished like hell this was a nightmare. "I trusted you and you went behind my back and did this."

"I was trying to help, Miles. I swear it." Quinn reached for him, but Miles jerked back, pinned him with a stare so hard that Quinn didn't move.

He'd dropped his towel to the floor and stood there naked and wet with those soft fucking eyes that pulled Miles in.

"No." He shook his head. He couldn't forget this. He turned to walk away, but Quinn was right behind him.

"Let me explain, Miles. The other night, when you told me

you wanted to look, that it's the one thing you didn't have the guts do to—"

"Me!" Miles slammed a hand against his chest. "Me. My choice."

"I was afraid of what you'd find! I just kept think-ing…what if you looked and didn't like what you found. What if it wasn't what you thought? I was trying to help. I wanted to be prepared so that I could support you. I wouldn't have told you anything you didn't want to know. I was just…*Fuck*." Quinn ran a hand through his hair. "I was wrong. I just…I wanted to give you something. You're hurting, baby. I see it in your eyes every day. You haven't let it go and, I thought…" He wiped his eyes. Miles saw the wetness there and realized his own eyes were brimming over too.

He was crying. When was the last time he'd cried?

"I don't know what I thought." Quinn stepped clos-er…then closer again. "I shouldn't have done it. I should have waited for you but I didn't and I can't change that. I just…I wanted you to be happy."

"I was happy," Miles told him. "Happier than I've ever been. But this? I can't forgive this, Quinn."

He turned and walked out of the room. Quinn was behind him, following him. Just as Miles reached the door, he grabbed Miles's arm from behind.

"Please don't go. I'm sorry. I'm so fucking sorry, just…please don't leave me, Miles."

Miles closed his eyes. Tried to block out the voice in his head that told him to turn around, to look at Quinn and pull him close…but he couldn't. He knew he fucking couldn't.

"You had no right," he said again.

"Please, Miles. Don't go."

Miles opened his eyes, tried to see through the tears. Once he wiped them away, he pulled the door open and stepped out.

"Miles!" Quinn called after him. "I'm sorry. Please, talk to me. I love you."

Miles kept going, knew Quinn couldn't follow him because he was naked.

When he got to his car and slammed the door, he let the tears flow freely.

Quinn had betrayed him.

Thea Jane Clements.

His mom, the woman who'd thrown him away was named Thea Jane Clements.

CHAPTER TWENTY-SEVEN

"**F**UCK!" QUINN YELLED, thought about chasing after Miles, clothes be damned, but then rushed to his room. His cell fell out of his hand so he reached for it again, calling Miles even though he knew there would be no answer.

What had he been thinking? He knew what he did was wrong. Knew it the second he saw the pain in Miles's face. The betrayal in his eyes. He'd trusted Quinn, trusted Quinn in a way he'd never done with anyone else, and Quinn had made a decision like that without talking to him about it.

He'd just wanted…fuck, to help? What? To save the fucking day? He didn't know. The only thing he *did* know was seeing the hurt in Miles had not been the desired result.

He dialed again. Listened to Miles's voicemail, his pulse trying to break out of his skin the whole time. "I'm sorry, Counselor. I'm so fucking sorry." Quinn walked over to the bed and lay down. "I think…hell, I think there was a part of me that wanted to be your hero? How fucked up is that? I wanted to be the one to take away the fear in your heart. I was so scared you would spend your whole life denying your need to find her, or that you'd look and what you'd find would hurt you even more. I told myself I was making the right decision, but I wasn't. I just…call me. Please. I need to make sure you're okay."

Quinn took a deep breath… "I love you," he said and then hung up and waited, hoping he didn't lose Miles for good.

MILES WENT STRAIGHT for the bar the second he stepped into Wild Side.

"What can I get for you?" Dare asked, a smile plastered across his face.

"Whiskey. Double. Two of them," Miles replied curtly and he could see the questions in Dare's eyes.

Still, he filled the two glasses. Miles took the first and slammed it back immediately. His throat burned as the liquid scorched its way down and he wanted it, wanted to feel something other than Quinn.

He tried to pick up the other glass, but Dare put a hand on his wrist. "Do you want me to call your boys?" he asked. Miles had come early, couldn't handle sitting around his apartment.

"No. I'm fine."

"Are you sure—"

"I said I'm fine," Miles gritted out, lifted the second glass to his lips and pounded the second drink as well.

"How much do I owe you?" he pulled out his wallet, but Dare shook his head.

"It's on the house, but I'm telling you now, you try to walk out of my bar, and I'm stopping you. I don't know what's up, but you're in no shape to leave right now."

Miles groaned, wanted to argue with Dare...but he was right. Miles knew it.

"How about you and I go spend a few minutes in my office. Would that be okay?"

No. The answer was there, teasing Miles but he surprised himself by nodding.

Dare told the other bartender he was taking a break before he led Miles to the back of the bar, through a locked door and down a hallway toward another locked door.

Dare pushed it open and Miles stepped inside, immediately sinking down in one of the chairs. He bent forward, elbows on his knees, legs shaking, hands on his head and looking down. There were footsteps that told him Dare moved, then the creak of another chair...and silence.

He was giving Miles leeway, giving him space to say what he wanted in his own time.

"What the hell am I doing here? I should go." But he didn't move. Knew he couldn't be in the bar right now. Knew he couldn't be around Chance, Oliver, and Matt—not yet.

Dare was somehow...safe.

"Can I ask you something?" Miles asked after a few moments of silence.

"Sure can."

"Why were you on the streets?"

"Old man was a bastard. Didn't want to take care of his son."

"Do you ever talk to him? At all?"

There was a roughness to Dare's voice when he said,

243

"Nope. Not once."

Miles assumed the reason was because his father had made his choice the same way Thea Jane Clements had made hers.

"I'm not saying that's right. There's no right or wrong answer to something like this. All any of us can do is what we feel is right for us and hope for the best. Why do you ask?"

"No reason," Miles replied.

"Bull shit," Dare answered.

Miles looked up then and made eye contact with him. "None that I want to share."

Dare nodded once. "I can accept that. I'm always here if you want to talk. Austin and I have taken a bit of a liking to you guys."

"Thanks, man. I appreciate it." He looked down again, wished he hadn't come here. Wished he could be alone.

"Do you need some space?" Dare asked prompting Miles to let out a relieved breath.

"Please."

Dare pushed to his feet, walked over and squeezed Miles's shoulder in support. "Like I said, I'm always here if you need something. Don't hesitate to ask."

The office was silent when Dare walked out.

Thea Jane Clements. His birth mom's name was Thea Jane Clements.

Veronica Sorenson would always be his mom.

He couldn't be here tonight, he realized.

But he also couldn't be alone.

It was only a few minutes later when Miles pulled out his

phone.

He hit Chance's name and when his friend picked up he asked, "Are you home?"

"Yeah."

"I'm walking over from Wild Side. Call Ollie and Matt and have them come over please."

"What's wrong, Miles? I'll come get you—"

"No," Miles cut him off. "I'll be okay. Just…call Ollie and Matt. I'll be there soon." He ended the call before Chance could argue with him.

When he got back into the main part of the bar, he found Dare and handed over his keys.

"I'm going to Chance's. One of us will be back for those."

He was in no shape to drive—emotionally, or with the alcohol he'd drunk.

"I'll take care of them." Dare shoved the keys in his pocket. Miles said thank you and then walked toward Chance's apartment. Two names ran laps in his brain the whole time, each fighting for his attention.

Quinn and Thea Jane Clements.

The woman who had given birth to him.

The one who'd thrown him away.

"Hey." Miles looked up to see Chance walking toward him. "Sorry, I couldn't stay home and wait. What's wrong, boo?" he asked.

Miles shook his head. Chance frowned but didn't push it. He threaded his arm through Miles's, locking them together before the two of them walked in silence to his place.

They went inside and Miles sat on the couch to wait for Ollie and Matt. This reminded him of the last time they were here like this, because Matt had broken Oliver's heart.

Quinn hadn't done that, though. Not in the same way, so his gut twisted in confusion. He couldn't make sense of it all and didn't want to. Not now. Right now he was too fucking tired.

It didn't take long for Matt and Oliver to arrive.

The moment they were all inside, Miles spoke, just wanting to get it over with. "Quinn and I are over."

"What?" Chance asked.

"Why?" Oliver added, but Matt didn't speak. Miles locked eyes with him, saw how Matt studied him, cocked his head as though he could look deeper that way, and Miles had to turn away. It felt too intense, as though Matt saw something in him the rest of them didn't.

"He betrayed me," Miles told them. But had he? Had he really betrayed him? It felt like it.

"He cheated on you?" Oliver asked. "That doesn't sound like Quinn. Are you sure?"

"He didn't cheat on me." He rubbed a hand over his head, looked down because the attention on him was too much.

"What did he do?" Chance asked.

"It's…" *He found my birth mother… I don't know how I feel about that… What about Mom and Dad?* "It's between us."

Chance opened his mouth to speak, but Miles cut him off, "It's between us," he repeated. He couldn't do this tonight. His brain was a minefield with so many triggers that were ready for explosion.

"I just…"

Oliver sighed. Was the first to walk over and sit beside him. Chance came next. Miles dropped his head to Oliver's shoulder the same way Oliver had done with him not too long ago. Chance wrapped an arm around him, but Matt? Matty just watched him, and Miles knew that out of everyone in the room, Matt somehow understood what he was going through more than anyone else.

CHAPTER TWENTY-EIGHT

Q UINN SAT IN his car outside of the LGBT youth center and didn't want to go in. He would do anything not to have to walk through those doors, but he felt as though he had to. Felt like it was the right thing to do.

Still, dread pumped through his veins. A heavy weight pulled down his heart and he wished things could be different. Wished everything hadn't gone down the way it had.

That he would have spoken to Miles first. That he would have let Miles handle his life in his own way.

That he hadn't been so damn afraid of losing him, that he forced an issue he thought would help when he didn't have a fucking clue. Everyone handled their shit differently. Everyone felt differently about their lives and choices and what was right for them. What Quinn thought was best, wasn't necessarily best for Miles, and he should have seen that.

Before he changed his mind and slunk away with this tail between his legs, Quinn got out of the car. He was five minutes late, which wasn't like him but considering he didn't want to be here, it made sense.

The receptionist smiled when he walked inside. She was obviously expecting him, but he still signed in the way he was supposed to before telling her he could get to Austin's office on his own.

When he reached the door, he saw it was open. Austin sat behind the desk as he did the last time Quinn was there. Oliver was in the same chair he'd occupied before too. He stood automatically and hugged Quinn.

"Hey, it's good to see you," Oliver told him.

"It's good to see you too." And this reaction? Oliver welcoming him like this meant every fucking thing in the world to Quinn. Their devotion would always be to Miles, as it should be, but he'd hated the thought that they could be angry at him.

For all he knew, maybe Miles hadn't even told them what happened.

When they parted, Austin stood and shook hands with Quinn.

"Is everything okay?" Austin asked as the three men settled in their seats.

No, no it wasn't. "Yeah," he replied. "I just wanted to let you know that because of a few new developments, I'm going to have to step down in helping you guys with our project. All my promises will still be fulfilled of course. I have the name and phone number of someone else who works with me, and they're incredibly excited to head up the tour of our facility. His name is Tim, and he'll also be in charge of the game day we have planned here."

Austin's forehead wrinkled. He likely had no idea that anything had gone down with him and Miles. "Is everything okay? I know how excited you were to work on this."

He really had been excited. He'd wanted it so much, but… "Yeah. I'm okay. And it's still happening, which is all that matters." The youths would still get every benefit they were before. Quinn guaranteed it. He just couldn't do this to Miles. He thought about what Miles had told him about the pacts and contracts and why he'd struggled with Matt. Quinn wouldn't be a source of tension between their friendships. The four men had one of the most beautiful relationships Quinn had ever seen.

"Quinn," Oliver started, but Quinn shook his head. He expected Oliver to try and talk him out of it.

"No. It's important I do this."

Oliver sighed. Austin told Quinn that he hated to see him go but he understood if it was a commitment Quinn could no longer make.

The conversation went rather quickly. Quinn didn't want to be there any longer than he had to.

He wasn't surprised when Oliver walked out with him. He wasn't surprised when he stopped Quinn in the parking lot and asked, "Why are you doing this?"

Quinn shrugged and answered honestly, "Because I think it will be easier for Miles." After the way Quinn hurt him, totally sideswiped him with information he didn't expect, being around Quinn or knowing that Quinn was working closely with his friend would be the last thing Miles needed.

"What happened between the two of you?" Oliver asked next.

He wouldn't give specifics. Miles likely wanted to forget

whatever information he saw on his mother. If he hadn't told Oliver himself, Quinn wouldn't be the one to do it. "I hurt him." He'd taken Miles's choice away from him, the same way his mother had taken Miles's life into her hands.

"Shit," Oliver cursed quickly, then locked eyes with Quinn. "Why do I have the feeling you're just as hurt as he is? That whatever happened wasn't intentional and your god-damned heart is breaking?"

Because it wasn't intentional. Because his heart was broken. Rather than answering Oliver, he asked, "How is he?" It had only been a few days since everything went down between them. Since Miles left work early to surprise Quinn and had felt betrayed instead.

"He's hurting too...not like he'll share it with us. You know how he is. He loves the rest of us so damn much that he couldn't live without knowing what pained us, but when it comes to himself, he just doesn't feel the same."

This time it was Quinn's turn to curse. "Fuck," he mumbled before running a hand through his hair. "Don't let him close in on himself, okay? Just be there for him. Make sure he knows he's not alone."

"He's never alone," Oliver answered.

"I know."

"Are you?" Oliver questioned. Was Quinn alone, that's what he wanted to know.

"I'm fine," he lied.

"Are you alone, though?"

Quinn shook his head. "I'm thinking about going to see

my best friend, Christian, for a little while. Just to get away."

Oliver nodded but looked a little sad. He frowned before he pulled Quinn in for another hug. "You're our friend now too. You call any time."

"I will. Thank you."

Oliver pulled away and added, "You look tired. Get some rest."

He was tired—both physically and emotionally. "I will."

He watched as Oliver walked away. Quinn had never felt so alone in his whole life.

———⌇∿⌇———

IT WAS SATURDAY evening.

It had been a week and a day since Miles walked into Quinn's apartment and saw what his mom looked like for the first time. A week and a day since he learned her name.

A week and a day since he walked away from Quinn.

He sat in front of his computer where he spent most of his spare time over the past week, the name Thea Jane Clements Sacramento typed out, but he had yet to hit return. He had yet to actually search for her. He'd delete her name, shut down his computer, only to open it back up and type the name again.

Why did he need to know so much? Why did the lack of knowledge eat through him every day of his life?

He didn't want her to be his mother. He had one of those. But he needed to know. He needed an answer he could understand, one that made sense.

That wasn't the only thing on his mind either.

He missed Quinn. He was this constant ache in Miles's chest. This need that coursed through him every second of every day.

But what he'd done had hurt.

Miles's eyes darted up when there was a knock at his door. It was close to seven. He wasn't expecting anyone, but that didn't mean much of anything. He'd been horrible company at Wild Side the night before and he wouldn't put it past his friends if he found the three of them standing there waiting for him.

He thought about ignoring it but found himself pushing to his feet. Found himself walking over. Found himself frowning slightly in surprise when he opened the door.

It wasn't Chance.

It wasn't Oliver.

But it was Matt. Alone.

"Can I come in for a second?" he asked.

"Yeah, sure. Of course." Miles let him inside, before closing the door behind him. "Do you want something to drink?" he asked, but Matt shook his head. The rigidness in the set of his shoulders immediately told Miles something was wrong.

"Is Ollie okay? There's nothing wrong with Oliver, is there?" His heart beat double time.

"No, he's fine." Matt turned to face him. "But I don't think you are. I don't think you've been fine for a very long time. I know because I was the same way."

"Fuck," Miles cursed quietly. He didn't like being called out on his shit. The instinct was there, building inside of him to tell Matt he was fine. To tell him to mind his own business…but he was right. There wasn't a part of Miles that didn't know he was right.

He'd been suffering in silence ever since he was a child, which made him feel guilty and weak because he had an incredible life. The best of friends. Parents he wouldn't trade for anything in the world. A career he loved.

He'd had a man he loved too.

Life wasn't always that easy though, was it? Maybe he'd been wrong all along and *one plus one* rarely made two.

When Miles didn't reply, Matt continued. "I used to get so upset with myself. I couldn't understand why I just wasn't happy. My life wasn't perfect, but it could have been worse. Regardless of how I struggled sometimes, I knew I had family who loved me. I had everything going for me. I had this beautiful man who would have done anything for me but I fought happiness, fought it because somehow, there was a part of me that believed I didn't deserve it. I realize now that I deserve it, and you do too."

"I know," Miles replied, because he did. He didn't believe he didn't deserve happiness. He was just… "I don't want to get hurt."

"Does anyone want to get hurt? Denying yourself is just a different version of pain. Believe me, I know."

He was right. Jesus, he was so fucking right.

"Quinn found my birth mother," Miles admitted. He walked over and sat on the couch, and Matt joined him. "He didn't tell me he was going to look. I didn't ask him to…but

God, I think a part of me was glad that he did, while at the same time, I felt betrayed. I was jealous because he had the strength to do something I didn't."

"That doesn't make you weak, Miles. That makes you human. You have fears and worries, just like the rest of us, and they're all different for everyone. And you have to remember, Quinn wasn't as emotionally attached as you. Is that what happened? You told him you didn't want to look for her and he did it anyway?"

He shook his head. "No. I told him that it was the one thing I'd always wanted to do but was too afraid."

So Quinn had done it for him. Quinn had tried to bear that weight. And no, it wasn't the right decision. It was and should have always been Miles's choice to make, but Quinn did it out of love. There wasn't a part of him that doubted it.

"Ollie said he stepped down from helping with the youth center. He's having someone else fill his obligations. I wasn't sure if you knew but figured you'd want to."

Miles's eyes snapped up and met Matt's. "He did?"

"Yeah."

For him. Miles knew Quinn did that for him. He was giving Miles his life but...he didn't want it. Not from Quinn. He really fucking didn't.

"I have to go." Miles shoved to his feet.

"I thought you might," Matt teased.

"Cocky son of a bitch," Miles tossed back at him as he stepped into his shoes. He took a moment then to look up at Matt and get serious. "Thank you."

"All I did was talk to you."

"Yeah, but you didn't have to. And I don't think anyone else would have been able to get through to me yet, other than you."

"I'm glad I could help." He shrugged, and Miles smiled at him. He shoved his phone into this pocket and grabbed his keys.

He needed Quinn.

CHAPTER TWENTY-NINE

MILES KNOCKED FOR the second time on Quinn's door. He'd seen Quinn's car out front, and even if he hadn't, somehow he would have known his guy was inside.

He didn't call out, didn't alert Quinn that it was him. He only waited, and when Quinn didn't answer the door, he pulled his keys out of his pocket and unlocked it himself.

If he hadn't known in his heart that he would be back here again, he would have gotten rid of it, but he hadn't because this was Quinn and his heart would always be tied to this man.

"It's me," he said as he pushed the door open. The apartment was dark. It was only a little after seven, but with the lights out and the blinds closed it looked later.

Quinn's computer screen was the only thing that glowed.

"Miles?" Quinn sat up. He'd been lying down on the couch, but as Miles walked over, he knew Quinn definitely hadn't been sleeping.

Not just in this moment either. He hadn't been sleeping well, at all.

He had a few days' stubble on his face. His normally wide eyes were narrow and red.

"Fuck," Miles gritted out as guilt flooded his insides.

"What are you doing here, Counselor?" Quinn asked.

Miles replied with, "Shh," before bending over and picking Quinn up. Miles lifted Quinn into his arms, holding him.

Quinn didn't fight him, which spoke to how tired he was. How long had it been since he'd had a good night's sleep? Christ, Miles should have known better. He should have checked on Quinn. He should have been there for him.

"I got you, baby boy," Miles said as Quinn wrapped his arms around Miles's neck. "I got you. I'm here." He kissed Quinn's forehead. Held him tight. In this moment, nothing else mattered—not that they'd had a fight or that Quinn had gone behind his back, even if it was to help Miles. The only thing he cared about was taking care of the man in his arms the loving way Quinn took care of his heart.

"I can walk, ya know?" Quinn said into his neck.

"But I don't want you to," Miles admitted.

"I don't want to either."

He carried Quinn to his bedroom, where he noticed the bedside lamp was on. When he set Quinn on the edge of the bed, Miles told him, "Arms in the air," and Quinn immediately did it.

Miles tugged Quinn's white tee over his head. His hair was drying. Had he taken a shower recently to help him sleep or to keep himself awake?

"Lie down," he told Quinn next. When Quinn did it, he hooked his fingers on the edges of Quinn's white pajama pants and tugged them down. "No underwear, huh? Were you expecting me?"

"I was hoping." Quinn winked, but his voice was almost hollow. Raspy and tired and damned if it didn't break Miles's heart. "What are you doing here?" Quinn asked.

"Taking care of my guy."

"I hurt you."

"We'll deal with that later."

Miles unbuttoned his shirt and let it drop to the floor. He removed his pants, but kept his boxer briefs on before climbing into bed behind Quinn. They were both on their sides. Quinn's ass against his pelvis. Miles wrapped an arm around him. Smelled his hair. Savored the feel of his skin. Jesus, he'd fucking missed this. Missed this man he loved so much.

"I was wrong," Quinn whispered softly. His voice sounded as though it continued to get farther away when he added, "I was trying to help, but it wasn't my place."

No, it hadn't been his place, but Miles also knew Quinn's heart had been in the right place. His heart was always in the right place. "Shh." Miles ran his fingers through Quinn's hair, kissed his temple. "Go to sleep, baby boy. We'll talk about it later."

"Thank you," Quinn replied, and then Miles was welcomed to the sound of nothing but Quinn's even breathing as he slept.

QUINN WAS SURROUNDED by nothing but warmth. Miles's breath against his skin. His firm body wrapped around Quinn's. He wanted to keep his eyes closed. To pretend he was still asleep or to let himself slip inside again so he could pretend everything was the way it had been before. Pretend a serious discussion wasn't about to happen.

That wasn't the way Quinn rolled, though. He didn't run from anything, so he opened his eyes, tilted his head up and saw Miles leaning on his elbow looking down at him. "You been watching me sleep this whole time?" he teased. "That's a little creepy."

"Fucker," Miles replied and then, "No. I slept a little bit too."

"How long have I been out?" Quinn asked.

"A little over four hours. You needed it. You need more."

"I'm good."

"You're a liar," Miles replied.

"I fucked up." There was no reason to hold back. No reason to stall. This conversation had to happen, and then they'd figure out where they went from there. "I know I screwed up. It wasn't my place. It wasn't my business. I took something away from you, Miles. I took your choice and I get that and I'm so goddamned sorry. If I could go back and change it, I would. We both know that can't happen, so all I can do is apologize and tell you I love you and I was trying to help."

Miles sighed and sat up. "Balls to the wall, huh?"

"Is there any other way to do this?"

He shook his head and a small smile teased his lips. "No, there's not." He rubbed a hand over his head. Quinn sat up too, and they looked at each other. He couldn't read Miles's eyes, and he normally could.

"I'll never be able to explain to you what it felt like to walk into your apartment and see my mother's face for the first time in my life. It was like being hit by a truck I didn't see coming."

"I know." Quinn could hear the need in his own voice. The sorrow. "I fucking know. God, I can't believe this happened. What was I thinking?" How had he thought this had been a good idea? Why hadn't he talked to Miles about it more? Let Miles go at his own pace? "I wanted to give something to you... I think...I think there was a part of me that maybe felt like I didn't deserve you."

This was true, wasn't it? It was crazy how you could do things sometimes, and not understand why until later. "You have all these people in your life who love you, Miles, and then I come along and yeah, things changed for you, but what did I do to deserve it? What did I give you? I think I wanted to be the one to protect you in ways I couldn't protect Kane, but all I did was hurt you. All I did was—"

"How can you think that?" Miles cut him off. "How can you think you don't deserve me? I'm not Kane, and you didn't fail him either. You've changed my whole goddamned world, Quinn. You showed my heart it was okay to fall. It was okay to let someone in."

"I did that?" he tried to joke, but Miles just shook his head. Quinn ruffled his hair with his hand. "Maybe I'm not as together as I thought I was."

"None of us are as together as we think we are. Every person in this world is a work in progress."

"Even you?" Quinn teased.

"Especially me. I ran away from you, baby boy. I knew what you did was wrong but I knew it was out of love. I ran because it was easier. Because there's a part of me that was still afraid of you. A part of me that still needed you to be *two*, but you're not and you never will be and I don't want you to be either."

Quinn's pulse sped up. His chest got so tight it was hard to breathe. Christ, he fucking loved this man. "The anti-two strikes again?"

"My anti-two," Miles replied.

"I will never, ever betray your trust again, Miles. I will never go behind your back. I will support your decisions, even if I don't always agree with them."

"Can you make me one more promise?" Miles asked.

"Anything." He would do anything to get Miles back.

"Can you promise you'll still call me on my shit, though? I need that. I'm not sure if you've noticed, but I can be a bit stubborn."

His cheeks hurt he smiled so big. "No? You? I never would have thought. I will always call you on your shit."

"One more thing."

Quinn playfully rolled his eyes. "You're getting awfully needy there, Counselor."

Miles reached out and cupped his cheek. He rubbed his thumb beneath Quinn's eyes. "I think you should talk to someone. Find a way to work through your guilt over Kane. As much as I love that even when you're struggling, you can sleep when you're with me, I might not always be able to be there…Christian, either."

Quinn knew it took a lot for Miles to mention Christian. Not because he didn't like him. He didn't know the guy, but Miles was protective over those he loved and so knowing Quinn had a friend who could give him something that Miles could too, wouldn't be easy for him. "Christian is my friend. I'm so fucking in love with you, I can't breathe without you. And yes, I'll talk to someone. What about you?"

Miles shifted uncomfortably but as important as this was for Quinn, it was equally as important for Miles. Maybe more.

"Yes," he replied, his voice rough. "I didn't have the courage to research her. I just stared at her name. I don't even know what you know."

"It's not a lot but I'll share it if you want. When you want."

Miles nodded. "Not now. Come here, baby boy. Straddle me and let me have that mouth of yours."

Quinn did as he was told. He sat on Miles's lap, wrapped his legs around his waist, and his arms around Miles's neck and then he kissed him. It had hardly been a week since he'd last had his tongue in Miles's mouth, but it had been too fucking long. It felt like an eternity.

Miles nibbled at his lip then swept his tongue over Quinn's.

Quinn groaned in his mouth, and Miles squeezed him tighter.

His cock got hard and Miles felt so fucking good against him.

RILEY HART

"I missed this ass." Miles's hands roamed down his back and then squeezed his cheeks. "You gonna let me in it? I need you."

"Yes." Quinn dropped his head back. Miles kissed down his throat, and Quinn's eyes rolled back in his head. "I need you too."

Miles flipped them. Once he had Quinn on his stomach, he pulled away from him and took his underwear off. Once he was naked, he riffled around in the drawer for a condom and lube.

Quinn heard the package open, as Miles suited up. He moaned and wiggled his ass when Miles's lube-wet finger probed his hole.

"So goddamned hot and tight." His fingers were gone then and his thick cock was pressing inside. Quinn clutched the pillow, bit into it as Miles filled him from behind.

Miles lay on top of him, his mouth close to Quinn's ear as he pulled out, then thrust forward again. "This is my ass. Never gonna be separated from it again. Say it, Quinn. Tell me."

"It's yours," Quinn rushed out, loving the stretch of Miles's dick deep inside him. "Never gonna be separated from it again."

Quinn knew there wasn't a chance he would last long. He shoved his hand beneath him and started working his own cock. Miles thrust over and over, the sound of their bodies slapping together filled the room.

Just as Quinn's balls let loose and a hot stream of come

shot over his fingers, he heard Miles call out, felt his body tremble and then go rigid as he lost himself to his orgasm.

It was a few minutes later, as they lay there sweaty and breathing heavy, Quinn's head on Miles's chest and Miles's hand in his hair, when Miles said, "I want to talk to my parents first. Then…maybe you can tell me what you found. Maybe we can do a little more research together."

Quinn's heart punched against his chest. "Yeah…yeah, whatever you want. Whatever you need but only if it's what you want."

"It's important. The closure. I need to get past it so I can focus on my future with you."

Quinn wanted that future more than anything in the world. "I love you, Miles. So fucking much."

"I know, baby boy." Miles kissed his temple. "I love you too."

EPILOGUE

"**O**H MY GOD, he gets a lot of attention when he dances," Quinn told Miles as they sat at their table at Wild Side. Matt and Oliver sat beside them. It was one of the few Friday nights where Chance picked up a shift dancing there. He never did on Friday nights at any of the other bars or clubs, but Wild Side was a different story since they would all be here anyway.

Nothing came in the way of their night.

"Yeah, I know. He fucking loves it too." Miles put his arm around Quinn as they watched Chance move. "He's beautiful and he knows it." He wore a pair of purple Speedos. His eyeliner matched and his chest sparkled slightly, a mixture of sweat and glitter.

"Is he now?" Quinn asked playfully, cocking a brow at Miles.

"He's got nothing on you." Miles leaned forward and kissed the tip of Quinn's nose.

"Well obviously."

"Cocky."

"Realistically confident," Quinn replied making Miles laugh. He remembered the first time Quinn said that to him months before. He had very good reason to be confident and Miles loved the fuck out of him for it. He loved everything about his guy.

"We'd have some real competition if Chance heard that," Matt joked. "The two of you are always going at it."

Chance and Quinn had become quite close in the past couple months. Quinn was close to all of them in different ways—Oliver because of their work with the LGBT center, Matt because he'd composed a song for one of Quinn's games, and Chance because they just clicked the way Miles had known they would.

Quinn fit in with all of them as though he'd always been there. Miles didn't know what he'd do without him. Luckily, he knew he wouldn't ever have to know what that felt like— not unless one of them didn't have a choice. Like Oliver, Matt, and Chance, Quinn would never walk away from him. They loved each other too damn much.

"I like giving him shit," Quinn replied to Matt, just as Chance fell down into a seat with them. Miles hadn't even noticed he'd stepped down from his platform for a break.

"You like to give who shit? Me? That's because I'm more fun than your boyfriend," Chance joked, and Miles rolled his eyes.

"You are not more fun than me."

"Only because I don't have sex with him." He waved his hand. "Enough about you guys, there's a really sexy guy over there who's been eye-fucking me all night."

"Well, there you go. You can show him how much fun you

can be," Oliver told Chance.

"That sounded slightly sarcastic, Ollie. Do I sense sarcasm coming from you? Are you guys really doubting my fun-factor?" Chance picked up Miles's drink and finished it.

"Goddamn it, Chance." He was always doing that shit.

"You love me." Chance winked. "By the way, when are you guys going to Sacramento, again? There's this dance show I want to check out."

"Next week," Quinn replied for him.

Miles and Quinn had already been to Sacramento once and Miles had too many phone calls to remember...phone calls with his grandmother, Thea Jane Clements. His mother had fallen in with the wrong crowd when she was fifteen. She'd been introduced to drugs not long after. The pregnancy had followed quickly after.

Thea had done everything she could to help her daughter, to get her clean, but drugs were powerful and so was the man who pumped them into her. She'd run away from home not long before Miles was born—apparently to Los Angeles. They don't know what happened from there. Had she thrown Miles out? The man who had traveled down such a dark path with her? Did they leave him behind somewhere else and someone else had gotten rid of him? Had they traded him for money for drugs?

They would never have the answer to that question.

His birth mother had come back home. Had been too fucked up to tell Thea where he was...and she'd overdosed not long afterward.

His grandmother had looked for him but had never found him.

She'd always wanted him, though.

And she loved him.

The same way his mom and dad, the people who'd raised Miles, loved him.

He looked around the table at his friends as they laughed and teased and drank.

The same way all of them loved him as well.

"You're looking awfully serious there, Counselor," Quinn whispered in his ear. "What's going on in that sexy head of yours?"

He'd spent most of his life afraid to lose the things he had right in front of him. Afraid to get too close and let people in because he was so damn afraid of getting hurt, when it was actually the fear that had slowly been killing him.

This gave him life.

He had a grandmother. His family. The people at this table.

And Quinn. Jesus, he loved the man sitting beside him.

Miles looked down at him. "Thinking about what I'm going to do to that sexy ass of yours tonight."

"Liar."

"Thinking about how much I love you?" Miles added.

"Another lie. What's going on with you, Mr. Brutal Honesty?"

What was Quinn going for here? "Thinking about how lucky I am?" Miles tried again. All were true. Each and every one of them… "All of the above."

"That's the answer I was looking for."

He always kept Miles on his toes. "Dance with me, baby boy," Miles told him and then stood, pulling Quinn with him. Quinn went easily, and Miles pulled him into his arms.

"What should I do to that sexy ass of yours tonight?" he asked in Quinn's ear.

"Whatever you want. I'm yours just like you're mine."

"Yeah," Miles replied. "Been tied to you from the start."

He'd be tied to Quinn always.

THE END

Note to Reader

Thank you for taking the time to read TIED TO YOU. I hope you enjoyed Miles and Quinn's story. I have to admit, I fell hard for these two men. I can't tell you how many times I found myself smiling or my heart racing while writing their happily ever after. Outside of the romance, one of my favorite things about this series (as well as some of my others) is writing strong friendships. The Wild Side crew would do anything for each other. Now, that doesn't mean they don't fight, but what friends don't? I'm really having fun exploring their friendships through these books. If you haven't read DARE YOU TO or GONE FOR YOU, I hope you'll consider heading back to Wild Side in the previous two stories. And soon, we'll get Chance. I'm excited to jump into his book.

Thank you so much for reading. It's an amazing feeling to be able to live my dream every day and I couldn't do it without you.

If you haven't signed up for my newsletter, you can do so HERE.
www.rileyhartwrites.com/p/home.html

You can also visit my website HERE.
www.rileyhartwrites.com/p/home.html

If you're looking for a sweet and sexy romance check out One Call Away from Felice Stevens

When a brutal attack from a jealous competitor leaves Noah Strauss, darling of the modeling world, physically scarred and emotionally damaged, he quits the runway to become a psychologist. Using his contacts from his time in the spotlight, he creates One Call Away, a radio show dedicated to gay men looking for love, advice or someone to talk to. But with secrets of his own and a mother who refuses to understand the career path he's chosen, the one person Noah can't seem to help is himself.

On a drunken dare from the senior partner's grandson, Oren Leavitt calls Noah's radio show, pretending to be gay. Only Oren isn't certain if he's pretending. He's left his strict Orthodox Jewish upbringing behind, but the guilt remains. Guilt that his actions have prevented his sister from finding a husband and guilt that he's failed his parents. Talking to "Dr. Noah" helps, and as he finds himself calling the man again and again, he knows he must be honest. But Oren is unsure if he's lying to Noah or himself.

For Noah, trust is paramount; he's been deceived in his personal and professional life and while he desperately wants to help Oren, he also finds himself falling for the sweet and tortured man. Oren is trapped: he risks losing his job and more importantly the love and security of his family but knows he can't hide if he wants to be with Noah. When unresolved heartaches from the past rise up to control the present, Noah and Oren discover that love often comes from the most unexpected places, and sometimes a call for help not only saves a life, it can be a new and beautiful beginning.

www.felicestevens.com

If you love sexy, emotional, May-December romances, be sure to check out Strong Enough by Cardeno C.

When a casual hookup turns into the potential for love, staid Spencer realizes he wants to build a life with vibrant Emilio.

When twenty-two-year-old Emilio Sanchez sees handsome Spencer Derdinger walking by his construction site, Emilio makes it his goal to seduce the shy professor. Getting Spencer into bed isn't difficult, but Emilio soon learns that earning the trust of a man deeply hurt will take time and patience. With a prize like brilliant, sweet Spencer on the line, Emilio decides he is strong enough to face the challenge.

Spencer is surprised when he's approached by the gorgeous construction worker he's admired from the safety of his office window. Acting spontaneously for the first time in his thirty-eight years, Spencer takes Emilio home. When the casual hookup turns into the potential for love, Spencer realizes that if he wants to build a life with Emilio, he'll need to be strong enough to slay his personal demons and learn to trust again.

www.cardenoc.com

Acknowledgement

As always, I have to thank my readers. I couldn't do this without you. I am thankful for you every day. Thanks to my family. You put up with a lot from me.

My beta readers, thanks for the input and my editors and proofers for helping me make it pretty. To the members of Riley's Rebels for always being there. Also, thank you to Sarah Jo Chreene for the gorgeous artwork.

About the Author

Riley Hart is the girl who wears her heart on her sleeve. She's a hopeless romantic. A lover of sexy stories, passionate men, and writing about all the trouble they can get into together. If she's not writing, you'll probably find her reading.

Riley lives in California with her awesome family, who she is thankful for every day.

Other books by Riley Hart

Weight of the World with Devon McCormack

Metropolis Series: With Devon McCormack
Faking It
Working It

Wild Side Series:
Dare You To
Gone For You

Crossroads Series:
Crossroads
Shifting Gears
Test Drive
Jumpstart

Rock Solid Construction series:
Rock Solid

Broken Pieces series:
Broken Pieces
Full Circle
Losing Control

Blackcreek series:
Collide
Stay
Pretend

Printed in Great Britain
by Amazon